How
to
Fall

How to Fall

STORIES

Edith Pearlman

Winner of the 2003
Mary McCarthy Prize in Short Fiction
Selected by Joanna Scott

Sarabande Books
LOUISVILLE, KENTUCKY

Managing Editor
Sarabande Books, Inc.
2234 Dundee Road, Suite 200
Louisville, KY 40205

Library of Congress Cataloging-in-Publication Data

Pearlman, Edith, 1936–
    How to fall : stories / by Edith Pearlman.— 1st ed.
        p.   cm.
    "Winner of the 2003 Mary McCarthy Prize in Short Fiction."
    ISBN 1-932511-11-3 (pbk. : acid-free paper)
    I. Title.
PS3566.E2187H69 2005
813'.54—dc22   2004006221

Cover image: *Icarus* by Alexander Ivanov. Provided courtesy of London
Contemporary Art.

Cover and text design by Charles Casey Martin

Manufactured in Canada
This book is printed on acid-free paper.

Sarabande Books is a nonprofit literary organization.

Partial funding has been provided by the Kentucky Arts Council, a state
agency in the Commerce Cabinet, with support from the National
Endowment for the Arts.

for the young Pearlmans
Jessica
Charles
Naomi

CONTENTS

ACKNOWLEDGEMENTS

"How To Fall"   *Idaho Review*

"Eyesore"   *Ascent*

"Mates"   *Pleiades*

"The Large Lady"   *Crosscurrents*

"Trifle"   *West Branch*

"Vegetarian Chili"   *Happy*

"Rules   *Witness*

"Home Schooling"   *Alaska Quarterly Review*

"Shenanigans"   *Ascent*

"Madame Guralnik"   *Midstream*

"The Message"   *An Inn in Kyoto*

"If Love Were All"   *turnrow*

"Purim Night"   *Witness*

"The Coat"   *Idaho Review*

"The Story"   *Alaska Quarterly Review*

Awards

"Mates"   *Pushcart Prize XXV*

"Vegetarian Chili"   NPR ("The Connection") Award

"If Love Were All"   Moment Fiction Award—Second Prize

"Madame Guralnik"   *Boston Review* Award—Second Prize

"The Story"   O. Henry Prize, 2003

FOREWORD

In Edith Pearlman's story "Signs of Life," two unremarkable women settle in a suburb outside of Boston. They nurture attachments, battle illness, and grow old. Eventually, we can be sure, they will disappear, and much of their lives will be forgotten. But Edith Pearlman suggests that experience, no matter how routine, will be spiced with singular adventures. And evidence of singularity is difficult to erase. No matter what these women do to keep from drawing attention to themselves, they will be remembered through the stories told about them, and the stories will give their audience the means to imagine what has been left unsaid.

Another unremarkable couple arrives in the same town. They rent the top of a three-story house on Lewis Street. They work and raise their children. Eventually they move away, and after they're gone their neighbors realize that much about the couple remains uncertain. Who were they? Where have they gone? Why do we care? We do care, Edith Pearlman insists. In her hands, the uncertainties surrounding the lives of neighbors and acquaintances are as intriguing as the scraps of fact and prompt us to consider what happens when the story is over. Even if we can't know what follows an ending, we can learn something about ourselves from the concentrated effort to understand.

Edith Pearlman manages to combine subtlety with extravagance, understatement with spectacle, drawing our focus to the eccentricities of those who would prefer to remain unnoticed.

Foreword

"They were not adventurous, no, no!" she writes. "Whenever someone suggested otherwise they raised four protesting palms in negation as if they were under arrest." Humdrum appearances fail to disguise individuality. Confronted with unexpected obstacles, these characters exchange the blurring comfort of routine with spontaneity and improvisation. They fall in love. They fall to pieces. They make secret sacrifices. They take daring risks. They wonder if they have lived justly, fully, completely. They ask themselves questions that challenge complacency. "Hell gapes for the merely empathic: that was what Bill was beginning to think."

Wide-ranging in her settings, from the stage of a television comedy to a pawnshop in Istanbul, suburban New England, London during the Second World War, and contemporary Jerusalem, Edith Pearlman gives us the means to imagine what is worth remembering. In each of these stories, she honors the simple strangeness of life—the distinctive oddity of sheer persistence, as in the portraits of the women in "Signs of Life": "They are old women now—remarkable at last, just for being so old, and for maintaining independence and health." Whether the characters choose to settle or move on, resume or change their routines, they respond to unexpected turns of fortune with passion that is as assured as Edith Pearlman's prose. Full of vivid, intricate, nuanced portraits, confidently focused, restrained and yet spirited, saturated with a powerful imaginative sympathy, *How to Fall* is a remarkable collection by a remarkable writer.

—*Joanna Scott*

How
to
Fall

How to Fall

"Fan mail!" brayed Paolo. "Come and get it."

Every Monday and Tuesday Paolo lugged a canvas sack from the studio to the rehearsal room at the Hotel Pamona. Until recently Paolo had been Paul. The change in name was going to get Paul/Paolo strictly nowhere, in Joss's opinion; but teenagers had to transform themselves every month or so—he had read that somewhere. After dropping off the mail Paolo picked up lunch for the television brass and brought it back to the studio. He told Joss that he hoped to become a comedian. The letters that came out of the sack smelled of deli. Some envelopes had greasy stains.

"Missives!" He swung the sack onto the round table in the corner, loosened its neck, and allowed some of the letters to spill out—fussy business, too many little motions; but Joss kept his mouth shut. He wasn't in the coaching game. Besides, silence was what he got paid for.

Happy Bloom had been rehearsing his opening monologue—

3

the one he delivered in a tuxedo, the one with the snappiest jokes—in front of the wide mirror between the windows. But when he saw Paolo he whirled, stamped, and called a recess. He loved his fans. He got quantities of letters, all favorable. He was "the New Medium's New Luminary"—*Time* magazine itself had said so when it ran his picture on the cover last December. Churchill was on the cover the week before, Stalin the week afterwards, you'd think Happy had conferred with those guys at Yalta. But Happy was bigger than a statesman; he was an honorary member of every American family. On Thursday nights at five minutes to eight the entire nation sat down to watch the *Happy Bloom Hour*... And on Friday nights, as maybe only Joss knew, Heschel Bloomberg, wearing a gray suit and horned-rimmed glasses, without greasepaint, without toupee, unrecognized, welcomed the Sabbath with the other congregants in a Brooklyn Synagogue.

Joss admired the funnyman's faith. Himself, he hadn't been inside a church in eighteen years, not since the morning his daughter was baptized. But he had graduated from a Jesuit high school; he had believed in things then... "I like the routine in the shul, no improvising," Happy told him. "The cantor's a baritone, not bad if you like phlegm."

The Heschel Bloomberg placidly worshipping on Friday night reverted to Happy Bloom on Saturday morning. Writing and rehearsals started at nine; he usually threw his first tantrum by ten.

But today was Tuesday—the show already shapely, the skits established. There'd be only a couple of outbursts. Now Happy settled himself at the table to devour his mail. Joss strolled over to one of the windows and breathed New York's October air. Happy

4

might snuggle with the country; he, Joss, belonged to this stony metropolis which kept forgetting his name, oh well.

"There's a fan letter for *you*, Mr. Hoyle," Paolo said, and did a Groucho with his eyebrows. He extracted a pale green square from the heap and walked it over to Joss, heel-toe, heel-toe, poor sap.

No return address on the envelope. Joss opened it. Slanted words lay on a page the color of mist. He brought the letter up to his nose. No scent.

Dear Mr. Jocelyn Hoyle,

I'm a big reader (though small in physique). Television leaves me absolutely frigid. I don't ever watch hardly. Those wrestlers— shouldn't they sign up at a fat farm? Happy Bloom smiles too much. Much too much too much.

But I admire your face. Your long mouth makes thrilling twitches. Your dark eyes shift, millimeterarily. Those eyes know hope. Those eyes know hope deferred. Those eyes know hope denied. Oh!

The Lady In Green

Joss looked up. "This is a fan?" he inquired of the city. He sniffed the paper again.

The second letter arrived the next week, on show day, at the studio—they rehearsed there Wednesdays and Thursdays. Happy was screaming at the orchestra; at the properties-and-scripts woman who held the whole enterprise together, she had a name but he called her the Brigadier; at the writers; at the cameramen; at Joss. Paolo came around, the sack of mail on his shoulder. Joss took the letter from Paolo and put it into his pocket, unopened.

The show went all right. They had a fading tenor for the next-to-last number leading into Happy's wind-up monologue, the sentimental one. Joss stood listening to the tenor in what passed for wings. The studio had some nerve calling this a stage, wires and cables all over the joint. He'd worked Broadway, rep, vaudeville; the worst house he'd ever played in had kept itself in better shape than the New Medium. The two circuses he'd traveled with were tight as battleships; well, circuses couldn't afford bad habits... *"Nessun dorma,"* sang the has-been. He was at the point in his decline that Joss liked best: ambition flown; to hell with the high notes; emotion at last replacing resonance. He wore a tux and make-up but he might as well have been naked; Joss could sense the paunch under the corset, he could imagine the truss too, oh, the eternal sadness of fat men.

They all had a quick one afterwards—Joss and the producer and the Brigadier drinking whisky, the tenor brandy, Happy his usual ginger ale. Then Joss ran down into the subway. Searching his pocket for a token, he found the letter.

Dear Mr. Hoyle,

Ho! I've found you! *Id est,* I looked you up in "Who's Who In American Entertainment." Also in newspapers in the New York Public Library.

You were born in 1903, in Buffalo. You've been an acrobat. So have I—in my dreams. You served in the armed forces during the War. You have a wife and a daughter.

Such calm lids, such haunted eyes. Your expression is holy.

I wonder where you went to college after that Jesuit high school. Who's Who doesn't say.

The Lady In Green

6

He'd been a poor boy, but they were all poor boys at the school. He liked every subject, history best. Father Tom's breathless oratory made history alive. Father Tom's eyes were green and moist, like blotting paper. The way the fathers lived, there behind the school ... a quiet, chuckling sort of house, with Brother Jim their beloved fool. Joss too would teach some day, history maybe. The Fathers mentioned a scholarship to the State University. But he came to see that it was not Father Tom's subject he loved, not even the teaching of it—it was the delivery. He loved jesting too: not jokes like Brother Jim's, not words at all, but glancing and by-play and pratfalls. So he had joined a troupe right after graduation, disappointing his mentors and breaking his mother's heart. Now this letter-writing individual wanted him to relive those times ... In the late-night uncrowded subway car he stood up, briefly enraged, and shook himself. A man slid uneasily along the bench away from Joss; who could blame him; in the black glass of the window jiggled Joss the crazed marionette. The window threw back his face, too: the face the Lady called holy.

When he got home he put the second letter on top of the first in the bottom drawer of the dresser, underneath his sweaters. He could have stuck it between the salt-and-pepper cellars on the kitchen table, for all Mary cared.

She was asleep, lying on her back, her thin hands side by side on the coverlet. She would have watched the program in the darkened living room, bourbon at her elbow, already wearing nightgown and wrapper. Already? There were days she never got dressed at all. Tomorrow, on their walk to the train, she would tell him about his performance in a flat voice. How the camera had cut him in half not once but several times. How it had dropped him

7

entirely during the production number. How Happy held the audience in the palm of his hand. How Joss had outlived his usefulness... but she wouldn't say that.

The specialists he'd brought Mary to always first acknowledged the tragedy of their daughter's condition, then suggested that Mary's attachment and grief were excessive. You *could* have a second child. You *should* have a second child. You are in your twenties, Mrs. Hoyle... You are in your thirties... You are not yet forty.

Hospitals had been tried; baths; insulin. Nothing made a difference. She had been a darling little thing with soft lashes when they met; but the small downturned smile on her pointed face might have warned him of her fragility... A second child? He had too many children as it was. He had his sad-sack kid brothers, he had his damaged wife, he had Happy. And he had Theodora, Teddie, his one issue. Every Friday they went to visit her. It was Friday now, wasn't it—he glanced at the clock as he wearily undressed: one a.m. In a few hours he and Mary would walk to Grand Central and take the train and get off the train and take a bus and get off the bus and walk two blocks. They'd come to the iron gate. The guard nodded: he knew them.

Teddie knew them. She made that hideous moan; or she covered her eyes with huge hands. Sometimes obesity seemed the worst thing about her. She wore cotton dresses made by Mary, all from the same hideous pattern—short-sleeved, smocked, white collared. The fabrics were printed with chickens or flowers or Bambis. Sometimes Joss felt shamed by Happy Bloom's drag— lipsticked face and fright wigs and bare masculine shoulders emerging from an oversized tutu, or yellow braids flopping onto a pinafore—but why should Joss feel shamed, Happy was the one who should feel shamed, big famous comedian aping big retarded girl. Aping? Happy had never seen Teddie. "How's your daughter?" Happy would ask maybe once a year, his gaze elsewhere. "The same," Joss always said.

Though she was not always the same. He sometimes sensed a change. The exhausted staff shrugged. "Not growth," one of the doctors warned, his English infirm; "not expect growth, no." Okay; but once in a while her unforgiving expression softened a little, or her vague look of recognition slid into an equally vague one of welcome. If she could only talk. Perhaps she understood, a little. When they were alone—when Mary had left for one of her desperate walks around the fenced-in pond—he told Teddie that he loved her. He held her fat fingers. He kissed her fat cheek.

"Hoyle!"

Joss took his place at the table with Happy and the Brigadier and the writers. They revised, argued, laughed. Every so often Joss dropped his hand into his pocket and fingered this week's letter from The Lady in Green. He knew it by heart—he memorized each one now, like a script, easy as breathing.

Happy Bloom's loud good humor—I guess the public wants it.

Happy and the writers avoided the raw subject of the recent War. But the Europe exposed by the War had inspired many of Happy's inventions—the British dowager, for instance; the French floorwalker; even the milkmaid who yodeled first and then warbled in Yiddish.

But you—the silent consort—are what the public needs.

The public needed the dowager's meek husband? The floorwalker's intimidated customer? The milkmaid's goat—a horned, garlanded, Joss-faced goat who raised itself on two hoofs and executed a double-flap and a shuffle.

I absolutely adore the dancing goat.

Happy and Joss would be wallpaper hangers this Thursday. Costumed in overalls they would lift a protesting clerk, chair and all, out of an office. They would heedlessly paper over bookcases, radiators, paintings. The rolls of wallpaper wouldn't match. Happy would disappear into a doorless closet to decorate its inner walls. Joss would paper over the recess. There'd be shouts from the imprisoned Happy, in a variety of accents; he'd sing a few bars of "Alone"; he'd sing "Somewhere I'll Find Me." At last his head would burst through the paper, that round loveable head: the teeth, slightly buck anyway, goofily enlarged; a multitude of curls spilling over the brow; the eyebrows darkened and the eyes kohled. While Happy mugged to applause, Joss's back would be turned to the audience—the silent consort, papering a window.

"The show was funny," Mary acknowledged on the train that Friday. "You were funny." Her smiled turned downwards as it had in her young womanhood—but it was a smile; it was.

Teddie, sitting, looked away when they came, and banged her forehead against the hip of an attendant. After a while she stopped banging. The weather was mild for January; they sat on metal chairs in the brown garden. The paint on his chair was chipping. At these prices you'd think... It was better not to think.

You know something? He depends on you! Maybe you depend on each other.

And maybe she too endured a mutual dependence, a marriage

of convenience, a spousal alliance like his with Happy. Poor Happy —overbearing mother, two greedy ex-wives, years on the circuit, years in radio; and then, at last, seized by the new men of the New Medium.

Joss was doing third lead in a musical at that time, playing a father-in-law. The thing was holding on. Demobilized servicemen liked it. People were traveling again: out-of-towners liked it. It gave him a chance to hoof a little.

Happy called him. *"The Happy Bloom Hour* needs you!"

"My face on a screen?" Joss said. "I can't see that. I was a flop in Movieland..."

"It's not the same, kid. This screen is just a postcard. People aren't looking for handsome on it. They're looking for uncular."

"What?"

"Like an uncle," screamed Happy.

"Avuncular."

"Sure, what you say. That turkey you're in, Joss...how long can it last? Television: it'll be forever. Us together."

Joss said he'd think about it.

"Yeah, think. I've got your schtick worked out already. You'll be mute, won't even have to smile."

Once, early days, they had a near-disaster on camera. A guest came on drunk; he flubbed, froze, fell over the cables, passed out. And one of the girls had a hemorrhage backstage and was rushed to the hospital. The props were in the wrong places because they had not yet found the Brigadier. They had to improvise an entire number. Happy wriggled into his tuxedo and pulled on a pageboy wig, blonde. Joss grabbed a tweed jacket from the assistant producer. He came on slowly, the love-struck, ruined professor; he

11

sat down heavily at the stage upright piano. He played "Falling In Love Again." The orchestra kept still. Happy leaned against the piano and sang the song with a Marlene accent, nice, W's and R's pursed just as Joss would have done them, corners of the mouth compressed. The wheeled camera came close and Joss saw that it was focusing on his own face and he squeezed out some water. The papers made a lot of them that week, Mr. Bloom and Mr. Hoyle, bringing sensitivity to burlesque, melding tragedy with comedy, mixing tears and laughter, all that stuff.

Dear Mr. Hoyle,
　　What an article, that one in the Post, telling secrets, all about Happy Bloom's writers, and the people who have quit, and the ones who have stayed. And the rehearsals in the Hotel Pamona. Fans will be hanging around the Pamona all day now, won't they?

The rehearsal site had been known for months. Fans already hung around. But unwigged and un-made-up and bespectacled, Happy Bloom was as anonymous in a New York hotel as he was in his Brooklyn house of worship. At five o'clock he whisked unnoticed through the side door, a revolving one.

　　I myself will be in the lobby of the Pamona next Monday, April 13th, at noon.
　　　　　　　　　　　　　　　　　　The Lady In Green

On Saturday:
　　"Lunch? Monday? *Out?*" screamed Happy.
　　"Can't be helped," said Joss. "You fellows work on the patter number—I'm not in it."

And then Happy in one of his turnarounds said, "My dentist is threatening me like the Gestapo, all my gums are falling out. Okay, *everybody* goes out to lunch on Monday. Paolo will kill himself when he doesn't find us. Don't bother to come back until Tuesday morning. My dentist will bless you, Hoyle... But we start at *eight* on Monday, not nine," he yelled.

Monday they did start at eight; and at quarter of twelve the gang skedaddled, kids on holiday. Only Joss was left.

He straightened his tie and adjusted his blazer in front of the big mirror. First position, second, third... He grasped the barre and raised his right leg, high. It might be a good bit: mournful male balletomaine. Would it be funnier in whiteface? Suppose he played a bum trying to play Ghiselle? A churchbell rang. He was so sallow. Still on one foot he let go of the barre and pinched his cheeks; he had seen Mary do that twenty years ago. He resumed his normal stance, left the room, shut the door, locked the door.

He rode the elevator to the lobby.

The elevator doors parted.

He stepped out.

On a chair beside a palm, facing not the elevators but the registration desk, sat a female in glasses. The forest green of her jacket and the forest green of her pleated skirt hinted more at uniform than suit. Her legs were bare. Her ankles were warmed by bobby socks. She was about fourteen years old.

He walked slowly forward. She had a bony nose with a little bump. Her dark hair was curly and thin. She was probably Jewish or one of those hybrids. He looked at the feet again. One laced shoe had a thickened sole and heel.

Her age had angered him; her defect turned anger into fury. It

13

was a familiar tumble. Whenever one of his brothers showed up at the door—just a loan, Joss, something to tide me over—he was only vexed. But: I have *kids,* Joss—when he heard that he wanted to kill the jerk, and then he wanted the jerk to kill him.

He paused, waiting for rage to peak and subside. Meanwhile the girl took off her glasses. He walked forward again. He slipped behind her chair. He placed his hands over her eyes. Unstartled—she had perhaps sensed his approach—she placed her hands over his. For a few moments they maintained this playful pose. Then he slid his avuncular hands from beneath hers. He glided around to the front of the chair and stood looking down at his correspondent.

"I am Jocelyn Hoyle," he said.

"I am Mamie Winn." Her gaze didn't falter. Her small round eyes were the gray of gravel. She put on her glasses again.

"You haven't had lunch, I hope," he said. "Tell me you haven't had lunch."

"Otto believes that young people should be introduced to alcohol early," she said to Joss across the booth; and then she said to the waiter who was inquiring about drinks, "Kir, please."

"Wot?"

"White wine with a splash of cassis."

"Forget the cassis, Mamie," said Joss. "Draft for me," he said to the waiter. Perhaps Cassidy's had been a mistake. He wondered if he could be arrested for plying a minor. He didn't know her age exactly; that would be his defense. He did know she was in tenth grade, the prosecution would point out. The waiter served the drinks... "Otto?" Joss inquired.

"He lives in the next apartment. From Vienna. The University

14

of Chicago is the only true American University; Otto says; all the others imitate European ones. So I want to go to Chicago." She sipped her wine, leaving lipstick on the glass. She had much to learn about cosmetics. "Is your daughter in college?"

"Thanks," Joss said to the waiter, who had brought their specials, both plates on one forearm. "She's in boarding school," he said to Mamie: the practiced lie. "Your penmanship is excellent."

"Oh, cursive. I practiced a lot when I was young."

"And your writing, too."

"I go to a private day school," and she named it. "On scholarship. We are required to wear a uniform." She fingered her pleated skirt.

"Ladies in green."

"Rich bitches." A bold smile. "So ignorant! *National Velvet* is their idea of a masterpiece."

She came from a large, loose, wisecracking family. "Happy Bloom could be one of my uncles." The men were sales representatives, the women salesladies, an optimistic crowd tolerating in its midst members who were chess players and members who were race track habitues and members who were fat and thin and good-natured and morose and peculiar—"My great-aunt walks the length of Manhattan every day"—and even Republican. She loved movies and gin rummy and novels. She had a very high I.Q.—"That just means I'm good at I.Q. tests," she said with offhand sincerity—and because of her intelligence she'd been sent to the green school. "The uniform—it's equalizing, that's good, it's a costume, that's good too..."

"Mamie," he said; enough babble, he meant. He leaned across his corned beef. "Why these letters. Why to me."

15

She reddened; it was not beautifying.

"A bit of fun?" he helpfully asked.

"At first. I thought, hey, he'll answer..."

"There was no return address."

"Answer another way, get Happy Bloom to mention ladies, or green. Some trick. But then, I don't know, I didn't need an answer any more. I just wanted you to read the words, to wonder. When you look out of the screen with that face, it's like a carving, you're looking for me, you're looking at me..."

"Yes," he soothed, thinking of the camera's red bulb, the thing they had to look at.

"At school, they all have boyfriends," and she was all at once lonely and forty, and nothing had ever happened to her and nothing would. "I love your silence," she said after a while.

"My silence—it's imposed."

"Everybody at home talks all the time. I love the way you dance."

"The silent character—Bloom made it for me."

"I love the way you fall down."

He had mastered the technique young, while still at the Jesuits. He had gone to every circus, every vaudeville show. He studied clowns and acrobats. And in the first troupe and then the second he spent seasons watching, imitating, getting it right. He practiced on the wire, he practiced with the tumblers. Never broke a bone. Learned how not to take the impact on the back of the head or the base of the spine or the elbows or the knees. Knew which muscles to tighten, which to relax... She said: "You make me want to fall, but with my, you know, I can't." She paused. "I *have* fallen," she

16

confessed. She took off her glasses. Her little eyes softened. Would she ever be pretty? "Actually, I have fallen in love," she said. "With you," she added, in case he'd missed her drift.

There were several things he could do at this juncture, and he considered each one of them. He could award her an intent, sorrowful look, he knew which one to use; and from his gaze and her flustered response there would develop, during future meetings, a kind of affection. Stranger romances had flourished. When she turned twenty he would be... Or he could talk smart: prattle tediously about the Irish in America, his hard boyhood, the Fathers, the early jobs, the indifference of the public, the disappointing trajectory of his life. Bore her to fidgets, push her calf-love out the swinging doors... Or he could offer to introduce her to Paolo, what a pair... Or he could pretend to get drunk and stumble out of Cassidy's leaving her to pay their bill. She probably had a couple of fives tucked into that orthopedic shoe.

He did none of those things. Instead he reached his hand across the table and gently pulled the nose, the nose with the little bump.

They lingered over their lunch and then walked the length of Fifth Avenue. Walking, she hardly limped at all. "I don't do sports," she told him. "Steps are sometimes difficult," she said mildly. They discussed, oh, the Empire State Building, and the dock strike, and Hizzoner: the idle conversation of two friends who have met after a long silence, and who may or may not meet again. At the subway entrance on Eighth Street they paused. He took both her hands and swung them, first side to side, then overhead. London Bridge is falling down. Then he let them go.

17

"This afternoon has been..." she began.

"Yes," he said.

She clumped down the stairs.

That Thursday they did a take-off on *On The Town*—they couldn't make fun of the War, but dancing sailors were fair game. A movie tapster danced with them, another guy on his way down. But the spoof was too short. Three minutes to go before the good-night monologue, signaled the Brigadier. So Happy said "Sweet Georgia," under his breath—they'd done that number together on the circuit a dozen years earlier, feet don't forget. It was a Nicholas Brothers routine, so what, they never claimed originality, Happy stole most of his jokes. The Brigadier said "Georgia" to the orchestra, and then she hooked the Hollywood fellow off the stage, and there they were, Joss and Happy, dancing, just dancing. Happy flapped into the wings thirty seconds before the finish, to get out of the sailor suit and into the tux. Joss kept cramp-rolling. He felt Mamie's gray eyes on him and his on hers. He double-timed into a leap, why not, and he kicked midair, heels meeting, and he dropped onto his feet and then slid down slantwise, perfect, thigh taking the weight, and now he was horizontal. The camera's lens lowered, smoothly following him; those guys were getting better. Elbow on floor and chin on palm and body stretched out and one leg raised, foot amiably twitching, Joss grinned. Yes: grinned.

"What made you smile, they'll get rid of you," griped Mary an hour later.

He touched her hair. So dry; you'd think one of her cigarettes would set it on fire.

"I was smiling at you," he said.

18

Signs of Life

They were not adventurous, no, no! An unremarkable couple. Whenever someone suggested otherwise they raised four protesting palms in negation as if they were under arrest.

They lived in a small weathered house halfway up Calderstone Lane, the street that winds from Jefferson Boulevard to the top of Godolphin Hill and rewards the climber with a view of the Boston skyline. Clara and Valerie frequently climbed their hill; also they worked, gardened, paid taxes, got together with their many friends. Most summers they traveled to a village in Spain they'd discovered just after the War, when they were first in love. Then Valerie had seemed to Clara as beautiful as a sculpted boy—taut as a boy, bold as a boy, eyes swiveling like a fascinated boy's, and occasionally possessed of a boy's slingshot-straight power to wound. Then square-faced Clara had seemed to Valerie as authoritative as a Roman aedile. Val remembered the pictures of aediles, or at least of their busts, in her Latin Grammar—municipal

19

grandees who supervised the building of sewers and roads in the ancient City.

Now Clara and Valerie were in their placid fifties. Each summer they smuggled in a bottle of absinthe, and on festive occasions treated themselves to a thimbleful. They enjoyed legal alcohols too, in moderation; and, also in moderation, tobacco, caffeine, and a smokeable opium they were sometimes able to procure—the year was nineteen sixty-five. Walking was their sole exercise, unless one counted spirited conversation. They made love, yes; but affection had supplanted passion. Valerie taught flute and recorder in the Godolphin elementary schools. She was assistant director of the high school orchestra, and she played with various amateur groups. Clara practiced pediatrics.

The illness—it was a mystery. Much that happens to the body is mysterious. Valerie experienced fever, fatigue. Her physician verified an infection. Medicines failed to defeat the infection. The fever persisted; fatigue became exhaustion. Clara and the physician treated her at home for a while, with a little corps of nurses. They tried one intravenous antibiotic after another. Valerie sank.

She was dying, though of what nobody could say. She entered a nursing home—that is, she was transported there in an ambulance, holding Clara's hand. She did not seem fearful or agitated. These things happen, Clara said bleakly to herself; all doctors are acquainted with inexplicable illnesses and inexplicable deaths. Valerie lay for two days in a room six stories above Jefferson Boulevard. Clara, standing at the window, looked down at the Boulevard's elms, themselves ravaged by disease. Valerie breathed deeply but infrequently. Her pulse was shallow but regular. Then she breathed less often. Her pulse became fainter. She died.

Signs of Life

She died at ten at night, in the presence of Clara and an old, kindly nurse. Clara borrowed the nurse's stethoscope to listen to Valerie's dead heart and the nurse's flashlight to examine Valerie's dead eyes. Then she said she would take a walk: she must leave this place that life had fled from. The nurse tried in vain to stop her.

When Clara returned she found the nurse, hysterical, and a Russian doctor, bewildered. Summoned to Pronounce, he had discovered the patient weak but alive. Vital signs concurred. The two women assured him that an hour earlier, respiration and cardiac function had failed. Recalled to Life, he finally wrote on the chart—he was of a literary turn.

Where had Clara walked, that fateful hour? Oh, around the Town. She trudged along the Boulevard. The trolley from Boston passed, lit up like a nightclub. It carried two passengers. Aimlessly she paused at one of the bookstores in Godolphin Square. The announcement of its imminent closing was pasted on the window. Walking again, she dodged several automobiles. She noted with sadness that Godolphin—once lively even at this hour, its stores open, its citizens strolling—was flattening into a suburb. Valerie too would have found this grievous... Clara sank onto a bench at a bus stop. She covered her face with her hands and wept for her beloved.

Godolphin's decline was one of the many things they talked about during the weeks of convalescence, in their bedroom, Valerie immobile on the bed like her own sarcophagus—the illness took its time departing from bones and joints—and Clara in the tufted chair. Their trees, lindens, were in full and fragrant leaf, and the light entering the room through them was as green as the sea. The robust furniture they had bought in Spain seemed to dissolve in this watery surround. Yes, a bookstore was closing, the elms were

21

dying, one of their friends had fearfully installed a household alarm. The Town was dead. But Valerie was alive! Could they attribute her revival to the various substances floating in her veins? They couldn't be certain, they didn't crave certainty, they planned to discuss the matter till the end of their days.

The nurse allowed herself to be quoted in the *Godolphin Times*. "There were no signs of life," she said. The Russian doctor was next. "Me, I never saw her dead," he declared. "I walked in, she breathed."

When her recovery was complete, Valerie returned to work. One evening on the way home she looked into the window of Nature's Remedies and saw an ointment called Val's. In the café next door somebody unfamiliar pointed a finger at her and somebody else unfamiliar nodded. Tourists: Godolphin's first. Then there was an article in a Boston daily; and then a new inn advertised its proximity to the place of miracle; and then a great number of enterprises opened all at once, like flowers which had been waiting for the sun.

"Faith healers! Two of them, side by side in that alley, they'll be strangling each other..."

"Which alley?" Val inquired, and dipped her forefinger into the pot of honey that gleamed on their breakfast table. So unsanitary; for she would lick it now, and then dip it again, and again.

"The alley next to the movie house, with the arcade."

"Oh, yes, kids smoke pot there."

"And some fortuneteller has hung out a shingle upstairs from the florist. Madame Kissmyaski. There's a new chotchke shop that calls itself Lourdes. The next thing you know we'll have holy Indians, chanting..."

"They're here already. Shaved heads, yellow robes. Clara, their music is extraordinary, Mixolydian, I think."

Clara groaned. "Godolphin will become a . . . Destination."

"Vaut le detour." Into the honey pot went the finger with all its germs. Into the curved mouth now. Clara stood up, glared at Val, kneed away her chair . . . and moved around the table, and bent to taste those sticky lips. Oh, my love, my living love: what we might have missed.

"Darling! You have a patient, I have a class . . ."

"They'll wait," loosening her robe, loosening Val's robe; and Val knelt; and Clara felt the lips and their honey.

During the next few months bed-and-breakfasts multiplied. Herb sellers unfolded tables on the sidewalks and sold twigs and powders. The Godolphin police were reluctant to chase them away. A new restaurant opened—*Mirabile.*

What could Clara do? She had a practice to maintain—she was, after all, their household's chief support. Besides, she loved medicine. One day at the hospital she ran into the Russian doctor. He was a cardiologist, it turned out. Over coffee he told her that his own practice was flourishing. "For years I nearly starved," he said. "Now they run to me, the congestives, the infarcts. And you know what?" and he leaned forward until his big nose almost touched hers. "A lot of them—I make better."

Well, a little notoriety; and then renewed confidence—Clara could explain it all. A few successes, more confidence . . . "I have been Selected," the cardiologist preened.

That night: "There's this Committee," Val said. "Erecting a statue."

"To *you?*"

"Well...of me. Don't frown that way, darling. I told them I wouldn't pose."

The Committee engaged a sculptor anyway—an art student willing to work cheap. She installed the statue in the park at the top of Godolphin Hill, and chiseled V-A-L-E-R-I-E into the pedestal. Clara consulted their lawyer, who said that a suit would be a waste of money. First names were common property.

Val's photograph was off-limits, though. Most undertakings were content to reproduce the Statue on their signs. But the Statue didn't really resemble her. A windswept woman in vague draperies leaned forward like a ship's figurehead, her hands clasped in front of her bosom in a prayerful posture that Valerie would have died rather than adopt.

"One of those talk programs wants an interview," she reported to Clara.

"Over *my* dead body."

"Okay, okay."

It was late at night. Val was already in bed, reading and smoking; Clara was struggling out of her clothes. She had gained weight during this confusing time. "Would you really like to be interviewed?" she growled, trousers halfway down her fat thighs. "Become a thing of the media? Belong to the public?"

Val blew smoke in that inviting way; amazing that an exhalation could accomplish so much. "I don't know," she confessed. "Mostly I want to belong to you."

"You already belong to me. *Mostly?*" The old arrow, Val could still fling it, straight to the heart.

"It may be that I owe a debt to people of faith," Val sighed.

If you want to talk about debts, thought Clara...but she held her tongue.

Val went on. "Willy-nilly, I have been touched by the divine."

"Balls. You are an ordinary woman who happens to have died."

Their gazes locked. Their twenty-year history seemed to float in the space between them, seemed to rock there, like a phantom child. And whatever would she have done without Valerie, Clara inwardly moaned while maintaining the ferocity of her expression, trying to anyway, apparently failing, for Val, no longer lofty, said, "Publicity would be a horror. I don't know what I was thinking."

"Well," forgivingly.

"You see, we musicians...we all once wished to be virtuosi."

Clara, who had still not stepped out of her trousers, hobbled over to the side of the bed and sat down and took Val's silken hands in her coarse ones. "Such a charming wish."

So Val refused to grant interviews. A few more businesses sprang up without her cooperation; they succeeded without her connivance. But whenever she shopped at the Farmers' Market, as she had always done (it operated every Thursday during the good months, in back of Town Hall), she was trailed by a little crowd, eyes glinting with excitement, buying exactly what she bought: arugula, mulberries when she could get them, strong cheese—she knew which dairymen managed to bypass pasteurization.

Val ignored these followers. But during the second summer the farmers bought a plaster-of-Paris copy of the Statue, which they planned to display each week in a different stall. "If you don't smash that thing," she said when she saw it, "I will push my collapsible cart to the supermarket at the other end of town, and this troupe will plod after me, and what will you do with your mulberries then?"

Several shoppers heard Val's threat, and one who came into the office with a feverish child reported it to Clara. Clara's pen halted briefly over her pad. Then she tore off the prescription and handed it to the mother. "You forgot to sign this," the woman complained.

At home, *"That* must have been a virtuoso performance," said Clara.

Val knew what she meant; of course she did; gleefully she handed Clara a brown paper sack. "From the farmers." Inside was the statue, in five pieces.

"My sweet sweet," said Clara, voice hoarse.

And afterwards, after the long shudders; after the brief slumber; after the playful coda, fingers idly stirring, Val said: "This was worth dying for. Though all I felt that night was that I was turning into..."

"Yes?" Val had not been able to remember, not until now. "Marble?"

"No... Something slurry, with stones."

"Macadam," Clara recognized.

The stream of visitors continued even in cold months. Some merchants argued for a parking facility. Clara led the opposition at Town Meeting.

"Don't thunder, darling," Val advised.

So Clara pleaded: "Let pilgrims travel in the pilgrim way," she said. "On two legs or on four." Her faction prevailed. The Town decided that instead of providing parking it would operate a shuttle bus, The Donkey. The Donkey made stops at the new Repertory

Theater, the Sculpture Garden, Godolphin Square, and the Fabric Emporium, which boasted no connection with the miracle but drew customers anyway, probably because of the quality of its merchandise.

Brown-skinned men born in Brazil drove The Donkey. The Godolphin school system made room for the drivers' children and for other new children. The high school orchestra thrummed with unfamiliar expressiveness. The Town soccer team won the State Championship; and citizens, popping corks in Godolphin Square, hugged people they had never even said hello to.

Ten years later Clara and Valerie still proclaimed themselves unremarkable. They worked, gardened, paid taxes, entertained friends, practiced their mild vices, made their annual visit to Spain.

That season they indulged themselves: they bought a case of remarkable wine. It came by ship. Valerie arranged to have it delivered in the middle of the night.

"I don't want to unbalance our local wine shop," she told Clara. "I'm still a bit of a trend setter."

And so, one October night, there crept up the hill an unmarked truck, pale as the moon. It drove around to the back of the house. Clara watched from an upstairs window. She felt the night's chill. Valerie was not wearing a coat, though. She was dressed in her usual combination of long skirt and tunic. She owned this outfit in a dozen shades of gray. It could have been the uniform of a religieuse; it could have been the signature costume of an advertising executive. She opened the bulkhead doors, and then crossed her arms over her chest, for warmth. The two strong men who emerged from the truck carted the case down the stone stairs and into the basement. They came up again. One tipped his cap. The other knelt on the ground and kissed her hem.

He did. He did that. He did that suggestive thing. It was different from admiring the Statue or buying mulberries. In the open window Clara wondered whether any past moment in her life was worth remembering or any future one worth enduring; for if Valerie had turned into a figure not to be exploited but to be revered, to be worshipped—maybe even to be assumed—then she would never lie beside Clara in a double grave with a single tombstone. Their dusts would never mingle.

The men left. Valerie raised her face. It was still the face of a mischievous boy. She grinned profanely at her lover.

"Oh, get yourself inside," barked Clara, and, in her relief, slammed the window so hard that a pane cracked.

In the summer they often sit in the yard with their few friends still living, under a plum tree which long ago stopped bearing fruit. Almost thirty years have passed since the night of the kiss. They are old women now—remarkable at last, just for being so old, and for maintaining independence and health, though Valerie has undergone several surgical scrapings of her colon, and they have lost count of the nights that Clara, too breathless to climb the stairs, has slept on the living room couch.

They talk, sometimes getting it muddled, of the past: the illness, the death, the recall. Mostly, though, they talk about other things. A yellow columbine striped in orange has sown itself in their yard. It reminds Valerie of a cat they loved; and she wonders about cross-kingdom matings. The boy next door has a rock band that practices in the garage. They listen, mystified. They read poetry to each other.

Signs of Life

Tourists continue to come, trolleying in from Boston, strolling under the flourishing maples on Jefferson Boulevard. These sightseers attend the repertory theater and dine in the restaurants. At Godolphin Square they buy books and old stamps and antique buttons. They journey to the top of the hill—some on foot, some on The Donkey—and walk around the Sculpture Garden. Amid new welded abstractions and rough nudes, the Statue gets little notice. But few visitors leave town without stopping at one of the booths at the bottom of Calderstone Lane and picking up a pot of Revive!, an anti-wrinkle gel, or a bottle of Godolphin Ardor. It's an oily purple liquid rumored to contain opium and absinthe and nicotine, and it tastes like resin; nonetheless, it's a favored souvenir. Some people even drink the stuff.

Eyesore

At the candy works—a rundown set of buildings near the unused railroad tracks—chocolate nuggets coated with lilac were still made partly by hand. That fossil factory! Franny got to know it when she was still working for the *Godolphin Weekly Times.* Everything—the tracks, the shacks, the unburnished machines, the women in pink dresses stained with brown—was exactly as it must have been seventy years earlier except that the current employees spoke Cambodian. Even two years after writing her article Franny could still smell the overpungency, a child's idea of a perfect birthday cake, sugar and chocolate only, who needs flour?

She was nearly invisible in those days. Nobody noticed her. The oblong face with bumpy features was about as memorable as a paper bag. The glasses made the face even more indeterminate. She owned half a dozen corduroy pants, brown like her hair and eyes, and six sweaters, likewise, and a few pairs of sneakers.

Franny began to step out of the shadows on a morning during

31

her twenty-seventh year when an article in a science journal caught her attention. The article said that an exceptionally thin new contact lens had been developed, a lens that could be worn by easily irritated eyes. Franny looked up at her shelf of detective novels and Balzac and wondered, not for the first time, what it would be like to gaze at something or even someone without the intervention of spectacles. She looked down again, and read the names of the research team, and saw to her unsurprise that they were associated with a Boston teaching hospital. She found through the telephone book that one of them maintained a private practice. She made an appointment.

The lenses felt good. "No itching yet," she wrote to her mother in November. When she went home for the Christmas weekend she bared her unmediated eyes to her family. Her mother said she looked nice, and her brother's wife mentioned something about make-up when the two of them were putting away the dishes.

Franny's great-aunt gave her two velvet blazers for Christmas, one plum and the other cranberry. She put on one of them over the brown dress she was wearing, and instantly acquired the higgledy-piggledy look of a bag lady. But back again in her Godolphin apartment Franny tried on the blazers again, over nothing. This time her flesh reflected the silken glow of the jackets' linings. Her breasts glistened like a sultan's mistress. Her newly exposed eyes, above all this brilliance, seemed vulnerable.

Franny remembered her sister-in-law's remark. She visited a cosmetic expert.

A few strokes of the expert's pencil produced glittering orbs and sensuous eyebrows.

Franny learned to use the pencil.

And now things happened fast. The world of low-fat diets and high-impact workouts was waiting to claim her. Back Bay department stores teamed garments in a tempting way—a skirt, a sweater, a cape artfully flung. Who could be blamed for wanting the whole kaboodle? A new wardrobe took shape within Franny's closet: pants and jackets and shirts, in various deep reds.

"There's an army of fashion consultants taking over the world," she told her boss one morning.

He looked at her appraisingly. He was in his early sixties. He had been publishing and editing the paper for three decades. On behalf of the *Godolphin Times* he valued Franny's almost-presence—he knew that people felt safe with her, that they told her things. Her feature articles took weeks to brew, but they paid off in circulation. She did straightforward journalism as well; she had covered vendettas in the Massachusetts Legislature and scandals in Harvard laboratories. He could send her to local fires and accidents. Now, he supposed, he could send her to fashion shows. "What color do you call that blouse?"

"Claret, I think. Maybe port."

"Are you being distilled?"

Franny laughed; and he noticed that it was not the old head-ducking whinny but a new laugh, eyes meeting eyes, lips turning up as if aware of something nice about the person she was facing. "I did get one outfit in earth tones," she confessed. "To be buried in."

"Yes, well, not too soon, I hope. I have an assignment for you. That new soup kitchen, Donna's Bowl . . ."

"Donna's Ladle."

". . . Ladle, it's attracting an Element, shopkeepers say. Homeless who take the streetcar in from Boston, and have a meal at the Bowl, Ladle I mean, and then beg our citizens for money, even badger them."

"Stemming, it's called."

"If you say so. Will you check it out?"

She nodded, becoming again the old Franny, self-forgetful, ready to search for a story beneath ragged details. Plain? Maybe; he didn't mind; he was rather a colorless man himself.

Franny was just beginning the article on stemming—had spent several afternoons aslant in doorways, watching the panhandlers— when a bigger story broke. There was a murder in Godolphin—the first of the century.

She got to the scene about fifteen minutes after the body was discovered. The police were already deploying themselves, and floodlights glared at the apartment-house vestibule where the body still lay. Franny saw her boss standing on the roof of a parked car. She climbed up beside him. She was wearing pants and a brown sweater and her glasses—it was three o'clock in the morning. Her notebook was under her arm.

They had a terrific view of the hair splayed on the tiled floor, the layers of coats, the blood.

"It's that derelict," said Franny.

"One of the Ladle's patrons?"

"She came to town before the Ladle," Franny said, not looking at him, memorizing the corpse. The woman had hulked around Godolphin for about a year. Perhaps Franny had seen her most recently yesterday, perhaps last week. She'd had yellowish skin and yellowing white hair and pale blue innocent eyes, and she sometimes sat on a bench in front of the library, holding a mirror between her upturned face and the sun, plucking her hairline.

Eyesore

Franny and her boss stood shoulder to shoulder on top of the car. "Lieutenant Suarez says she was robbed," he told her. "And then hit with a blunt instrument. Or vice versa. Do you want this story?"

"Yes," she said. "There's a mortified family somewhere."

He squatted as if he had a cramp, and jumped, none too gracefully, into the street. He didn't offer to help her down. He was gallant by nature, but he knew his limitations.

Franny found out that the murdered bag lady had been the bedeviled daughter of a respectable family. The shamed relatives wanted to hide, to gag themselves, to burrow into the ground . . . to talk. They talked to Franny. Wearing the earth-toned garments, Franny sat in the New Hampshire home of the victim's sister, noting photographs, houseplants, needlepoint: trophies of a tended life. An ancient mother mutely quivered in a plush chair.

". . . never right, brilliant though she was. Brilliant! No one could manage her." The sister's fingers rested on her cheekbones and her thumbs curled under her jaw as if she wanted to remove her head with her own hands and hurl it into the fireplace. "The time I found her with no clothes on sitting in the basement washtub. She killed Dad, her doings did. Ma might as well be dead." The surviving parent trembled faster. "You understand," the sister told Franny, hot-breathed.

Franny supposed she did understand. Mostly she saw. She saw a child, confused by patterns to begin with, becoming terrified by embroidered flowers that seemed to move and a rug whose coil was striped. And those normal souls who happened to be the crazy girl's family—Franny saw them rigidly watching her hinges loosen and her lid pop off: how could she scream like that?

The editor of a national monthly magazine followed Franny's

series on the murder victim and her family. Then the editor telephoned with an assignment.

Franny's boss said, "Of course you can have a month off."

"I'm afraid she expects something urgent and despairing about city life," said Franny.

It was he who was despairing. But: "The assignment sounds pretty open to me," he said. "What's that stuff in your bangs?"

"Mousse."

Whatever the editor of the monthly expected, what she got was Gills. Franny wrote about a tuxedoed waiter, huge as a Nubian king, hurtling home on the midnight subway. And a French-speaking fish-broker, waiting at dawn on the glistening wharf. And a three-shift Pakistani family, some of them sleeping, some eating, some minding the store.

"We'll run it," said the editor. "But the title?"

"The adaptations of the hopeful," explained Franny.

She wore her new clothing and make-up whenever she went out during the day. But at home, and in the evenings, she still reverted to the dull old clothes and the naked face.

One night, at the twenty-four-hour grocery in Godolphin Square, she noticed a Russian émigré. They were all over town; even before she heard the accented speech she could always recognize Russians by the lined, homely faces and the hair that was washed once a week. Moscovites, most of them. She'd do a piece, some day.

The man in the store was about forty. He was buying cigarettes. She tailed him. His shoulders were stooped during the first part of the walk, but as the street climbed the hill he took on the jauntiness of a boulevardier, and by the time he settled himself on a metal bench at the top of Godolphin Hill she wouldn't have been surprised if he'd snapped his fingers and caused a waiter to materialize. Instead, solitary and grand, he lit one of his new cigarettes. Like royalty he gazed down at his domain. Franny crouched in a sandbox and gazed at him. The Russian smoked a second cigarette at one-twenty, and a third at quarter past three. Then he walked down the hill, slumping as it slumped, until he reached his rooming house.

Gills was published in the fall. A week later Franny received a telephone call from the producer of the local PBS news show, *Quidnunc*. *Quidnunc* wanted to interview her about other corners she'd found while creeping about the city as if on all fours; about what else she had seen with those eyes at the back of her head.

Ramsay Magraw, the dominant anchor of *Quidnunc*, was a rumpled slope of a man, his skin pitted, his irises the color of hemp. "We can talk about whatever you want to talk about," he said. Then he told her what to want to talk about. "General libertarian utilitarian egalitarian principles should inform your conversation. Vignettes to support them are always welcome. Did your iced bag lady have a right to be rescued? Did she have a right to be crazy? What's crazy, when you snuggle down beside it? Be intimate and deep, that's the ticket. Keep the fans always in mind." He looked down at his thighs, bulging in checked pants. "I love the fans, actually."

"Why?"

"They love me."

The anchors' desks stood on a low round platform, lit queerly from the circumference. The cameras trained their lenses on the desks. Beyond this cleansed battleground, in the shadows, Franny saw backstage debris: ropes, cables, hooks, boxes, a flung book, some bottles, stacked folding chairs.

"Wow," drawled the director after the interview, "what an exotic pairing, alert observer plays off deep thinker, we'll have to do this again. Call you?"

That meant good-bye, Franny figured. But no; she was invited to be a guest again, and then again.

"Are you getting paid for this?" asked her boss.

"No. Should I be?"

"I don't know."

All of a sudden Ramsay's co-anchor gave notice. "She's decided to stay home with her three daughters," Ramsay groaned to Franny. "I can no longer keep abreast of theories of child development. Won't those kids grow up deprived, without day care?" He fixed her with his manila eye. "Do you have children?"

Franny got the offer the next day, in the newsroom. It was not tactful of Ramsay to call her there, but it was politic. She could look around at what she was being invited to leave—the desks jammed together, the anemones drooping in clouded water, the boss behind the glass partition, the obese secretary who knew everything, the staff tippler... "I'll have to think it over," she lied.

Three days later, in the middle of the afternoon, she and her boss walked up Godolphin Hill. They reached the top, and settled themselves on the same bench the Russian had occupied.

"Summits," said Franny.

"I distrust them."

"Pseudo-clarifying," she agreed.

They talked of her new job. "An opportunity," he said. "Also an honor."

"I was on the spot at the right time," she explained.

"Fortune favors the brave," he reminded her.

Sunlight made her gold earrings sparkle and warmed her carefully blended make-up. The bench they sat on was cruel to his ageing buttocks. But in crepe trousers Franny lounged like a dandy. Her right foot, caressed by a pink suede shoe as if by a loving hand, rested on her left knee.

"I'll miss the newspaper," she said.

"But you'll like the tube," he said. "And the tube will like you back."

She didn't answer. This gentle man had hoped to teach Latin but had dutifully taken over the family publishing business. She knew that the wry face he was making, apparently because he could not suppress his distaste, was in fact a sign of vigorous self-control. He wanted to pull his hair out. Or hers. Or spank her, maybe.

She had rarely watched TV, not because the programs were offensive—content seemed irrelevant—but because the activity bored her. Now the thing was to become her livelihood.

She bought a VCR for her set. She took the *Quidnunc* tape home the night of her debut as an anchor. She slid it into the machine. In the unlit apartment her brilliant garments merged with the darkness. She sat on a hassock, elbows on knees, chin on knuckles. She watched herself. Then, forgetting the remote, she reached forward and rewound, staring at the spinning green numbers as if she could keep track of them. She watched herself again, then again. Content still didn't matter. She studied her face.

What a peculiar mug! The mirror in the bathroom didn't begin to catch its oddities—the touching slant of the jaw when she made a certain turn, for instance, or the way the moussed hair got separated by the tip of the ear thrusting palely upwards. Mirrors threw back only two things: the greedy stare of one eye as a line was drawn across the lid; and the preen of a finished full-face . . . Was that spittle in the corner of her mouth? She leaned forward like an anxious mother, one hand floating in front of the screen as if it could wipe away the dot of silver. The dot disappeared by itself.

She got used to her features. In a few weeks she was working on expression—still sitting on the hassock in the dark, head in hands, still treating the person on the screen as something to be studied. A thoughtful sympathy quivered on its face when it reported unhappy news. There was a friendly frown of exasperation when it gave some example of human silliness. But the chin lifted a bit too readily when a guest started to preach. Better to appear chastised; let the audience get mad on your behalf. And don't laugh at your own jokes, she directed the woman in the frame. She was its mentor now as well as its chronicler. You! You with the bump on the nose and the cantilevered lower lip. You're not attractive, you know—you only look attractive. She laughed at that unvoiced quip, or half-laughed; her left fist was embedded in her left cheek and only the right side of her mouth was able to smile. She wondered whether asymmetry would be captivating.

After a few weeks she stopped being critical. Now when she played herself at night she watched with admiration as her glossed, eye-lined lids rose and fell. Her frosted mouth grinned in the new crooked way. She was not so much at ease as accustomed. And cleverness had leaped into her mouth like a gremlin. She had put aside the metaphors she was accustomed to use and had taken up

40

instead the *bon mot*. "A man to be fecund with," she sighed after a report on a young millionaire. "She snoops to conquer"—that was how she summed up a luminary of network news.

"Your remarks have become pointed," said her old boss at their weekly lunch.

"Like pencils?"

"Darts."

"I do miss you," she said softly.

But his place in her world had been taken, not by the affected Ramsay Magraw, but by the two steady cameras, each with its glass lens and red light, scrupulously in attendance.

And people were beginning to recognize her. She who had been indistinguishable from her surroundings now stood out in colorful relief. "The TV lady, right?" She wondered if that Russian was a *Quidnunc* fan. He'd prefer the networks, wouldn't he? all those conflagrations in all those other places. On the other hand, public television supposedly stretched the mind. "We must expect that what we believe to be right will soon be proved wrong," she said, uncharacteristically solemn, quoting but not citing Max Weber, imagining the man from Moscow watching her in his solitary room. He lit another cigarette. She put her fingers to her lips in the un-self-consciously thoughtful way she had been practicing; she let the fingers slide to her lap, as if remembering all of a sudden that she was on camera; the right side of her face lifted in her trademark grin.

It was a sweet moment, she thought, playing the tape an hour later. Now she was the Russian. She tilted a pen between fingers and took an occasional puff, and watched the credits unscroll over a long shot of two anchors soundlessly chatting, Ramsay disheveled, she running her hand through her hair, she knew exactly how to do it, three fingers began at the corner of the brow and danced lightly to the crown, the bangs fell back perfectly into place.

It was perhaps too sweet a moment. She was never to achieve that repletion again. She began to feel gorged instead. Some days she shuddered with nausea, as if a substance was poisoning her and she couldn't stop ingesting it. ("We can't bear the stuff," the Cambodian women at the candy factory had told her. "We snack on celery and rice cakes.")

What disgusted Franny was the endless self-care. She resented counting grams of fat. She hated working out. She begrudged the time spent shopping for clothes. Mostly she felt tyrannized by the need to make up... she confessed this to her old boss over the telephone; she was too busy for lunch. "Painting the same pale egg of a face, morning after morning," she said. She didn't tell him that she now recoiled from the unpainted egg—not an egg at all, really: a beige lump, expressionless unless you counted the morning pout. Sometimes she was too hasty: her hand would slip and a clownish crescent would appear over an eye, and she'd have to wipe the stuff off with baby oil and wait for the oil to dry and start again. "I'm going to try surgical tattooing."

It was a new method of outlining the eyes, she explained to him, a method approved by the FDA but not by third parties. "Insurance plans won't have anything to do with this operation. You have to pay out of your pocket. Not to mention through your nose." She giggled. "Maybe I should do my nose at the same time."

"Don't touch the nose." Restraint had been his only tone-of-

42

voice for so many years; now he found he could summon no other. He tried repetition. "Don't touch the nose. Don't get tattooed."

She left her nose alone. She hadn't really been considering rhinoplasty; she'd just been making conversation. But she wanted the tattooing. It was her destiny, like the contact lenses.

She scheduled the procedure for a Friday morning—Ramsay would do the show without her that night.

The reception area was mauve. She was led into a very bright room with a recliner, and after she had made herself comfortable a plastic sheet was slung across her body and tied behind her neck. Then the recliner was tipped backwards and the tattooist came in, very tall, gowned and masked in green. A cone was applied to her nose—she had agreed to this, she remembered—and for some portion of time, not measurable, she floated in a vitreous bliss. The lordly tattooist concentrated on his millimeter of skin. Franny's hands grasped her own elbows in an enchanted embrace.

The procedure ended. The ecstasy faded. Her eyes were now permanently beautiful, or would be, once the slight swelling had gone down. She could get the eyebrows done too, the tattooist informed her. Lips were an entirely other matter—that was real surgery, the Paris mouth they called it, Hollywood hopefuls all wanted to look like Michelle Pfeiffer, it cost them a fortune, and they still had to wear lipstick anyway. Ever think of having those ears pinned back? You could mention my name on your show, I hear you have a show, never have caught it myself—cable's my game.

A week later Franny got an infection of the eyelashes.

"Palpebritis," she informed the camera, the audience, the

43

Russian, herself, grinning crookedly, her right eye gorgeous behind its contact lens, her left one squinting under the outraged lid.

She stopped the tape. PAUSE said the letters; the numbers were still. The infected lid looked warm. It *was* warm; a crockpot for bacteria. The asymmetrical mouth looked wretched. The moussed hair surrounding the besieged face could have passed for barbed wire.

PLAY. The homuncula—femincula?—oh, who cared?—continued with the news.

Things happened fast this time, too. Franny's right sclera developed sympathetic conjunctivitis. Now she looked as if a rival had been scratching her eyes out.

There were drops for the pain and drops for the inflammation and drops to correct the blurring. "Your eyes will heal," said the ophthalmologist. "But, my dear, tattooing... Really, I wish you had consulted me first. Of course you can't wear your lenses."

Eyeglasses quenched Franny's new face. She tried the standard frames she'd worn when she worked for the newspaper. Perhaps she looked no plainer now than earlier; but she had become accustomed to distinctiveness. She tried grannies and goggles and harlequins. Nothing helped.

She couldn't manage the lopsided smile.

She became too uneasy to run her hand through her hair.

The nervous wit pried itself loose from her tongue and ran off.

She felt her charm draining away, like life. And everybody at *Quidnunc* was so noticeably kind, to her face, and so patently engaged in sabotage, behind her back.

When Ramsay told her that the contract wouldn't be renewed;

that her predecessor, driven crazy by the kids, wanted the old job back, Franny shrugged inside a brown sweater. "I was not cut out to be an anchor," she said at last.

"No? What were you cut out for, then?" shuffling some papers.

An anchorite ... But she wouldn't waste the pun on him.

She is good at free-lance editing, but the pay is skimpy. Her eyes have recovered. She walks up Godolphin Hill most nights. She thinks about the bag lady a lot, she told her boss at their most recent lunch. "Maybe I should study social work," she mused. "Or become a cop." He didn't reply. Suddenly animated, she said, "I'll take up stemming. I'll wear shades and a cardboard sign. Seduced and Abandoned!" and for a forgetful moment, she lifted one corner of her mouth.

Mates

Keith and Mitsuko Maguire drifted into town like hoboes, though the rails they rode were only the trolley tracks from Boston, and they paid their fares like everyone else. But they seemed as easy as vagabonds, without even a suitcase between them, and only one hat, a canvas cap. They took turns putting it on. Each wore a hiker's back frame fitted with a sleeping bag and a knapsack. Two lime green sneakers hung from Mitsuko's pack.

That afternoon they were seen sharing a loaf and a couple of beers on a bench in Logowitz Park. Afterwards they relaxed under a beech tree with their paperbacks. They looked as if they meant to camp there. But sleeping outside was as illegal twenty-five years ago as it is today; and these newcomers, it turned out, honored the law. In fact they spent their first night in the Godolphin Inn, like ordinary travelers. They spent their second night in the apartment they had just rented at the top of a three-decker on Lewis Street, around the corner from the house I have lived in since I was a girl.

47

And there they stayed for a quarter of a century, maintaining cordial relations with the downstairs landlord and with the succession of families who occupied the middle flat.

Every fall they planted tulips in front. In the spring Keith mowed the side lawn. Summers they raised vegetables in the back; all three apartments shared the bounty.

Anyone else in their position would have bought a single-family house or a condo, maybe after the first child, certainly after the second. Keith, a welder, made good money; and Mitsuko, working part time as a computer programmer, supplemented their income. But the Maguires kept on paying rent as if there were no such thing as equity. They owned no television; and their blender had only three speeds. But although the net curtains at their windows seemed a thing of the moment, like a bridal veil, their plain oak furniture had a responsible thickness. On hooks in the back hall hung the kids' rain gear, and Keith's hard hat, and Mitsuko's sneakers. The sneakers' green color darkened with wear; eventually she bought a pair of pink ones.

I taught all three of the boys. By the time the oldest entered sixth grade he was a passionate soccer player. The second, the bookish one, wore glasses. The third, a cutup, was undersized. In each son the mother's Eastern eyes looked out of the father's Celtic face; a simple, comely, repeated visage; a glyph meaning 'child.'

Mitsuko herself was not much bigger than a child. When the youngest began high school even he had outstripped his mother. Her little face contained a soft beige mouth, a nose of no consequence, and those mild eyes. Her short hair was clipped every month by Keith. (In return Mitsuko trimmed Keith's

48

receding curls and rusty beard.) She wore tees and jeans and sneakers except for public occasions; then she wore a plum-colored skirt and a white silk blouse. I think it was always the same skirt and blouse. The school doctor once referred to her as generic; but when I asked him to identify the genus he sighed his fat sigh. "Female parent? All I mean is that she's stripped down." I agreed. It was as if nature had given her only the essentials: flat little ears; binocular vision; teeth strong enough for buffalo steak, though they were required to deal with nothing more fibrous than apples and raw celery (Mitsuko's cuisine was vegetarian). Her breasts swelled to the size of teacups when she was nursing, then receded. The school doctor's breasts, sometimes visible under a summer shirt, were slightly bigger than Mitsuko's.

The Maguires attended no church. They registered Independent. They belonged to no club. But every year they helped organize the spring block party and the fall park clean-up. Mitsuko made filligree cookies for school bake sales and Keith served on the search committee when the principal retired. When their eldest was in my class, each gave a What-I-Do talk to the sixth grade. At my request they repeated it annually. Wearing a belt stuffed with tools, his mask in his hands, Keith spoke of welding's origins in the forge. He mentioned weapons, tools, automobiles. He told us of the smartness of the wind, the sway of the scaffolding, the friendly heft of the torch. "An arc flames and then burns blue," he said. "Steel bar fuses to steel bar." Mitsuko in her appearances before the class also began with history. She described Babbage's first calculating machine, whose innards nervously clacked. She recapitulated the invention of the Hollerith code (the punched card she showed the kids seemed as venerable as papyrus); the

49

cathode tube; the microchip. Then she too turned personal. "My task is to achieve intimacy with the computer," she said. "To follow the twists of its thought; to help it become all it can." When leaving she turned at the doorway and gave us the hint of a bow.

Many townspeople knew the Maguires. How could they not, with the boys going to school and making friends and playing sports? Their household had the usual needs—shots and checkups, medications, vegetables, hardware. The kids bought magazines and notebooks at Dunton's Tobacco. Every November Keith and his sons walked smiling into Roberta's Linens and bought a new Belgian handkerchief for Mitsuko's birthday. During the following year's special occasions, its lace would foam from the pocket of the white silk blouse.

But none of us knew them well. They didn't become anyone's intimates. And when they vanished, they vanished in a wink. One day we heard that the youngest was leaving to become a doctor; the next day, or so it seemed, the parents had decamped.

I had seen Mitsuko the previous week. She was buying avocados at the greengrocer. She told me that she mixed them with cold milk and chocolate in the blender. "The drink is pale green, like a dragonfly," she said. "Very refreshing."

Yes, the youngest was off to Medical School. The middle son was teaching carpentry in Oregon. The oldest, a journalist in Minnesota, was married and the father of twin girls.

So she had granddaughters. She was close to fifty, but she still could have passed for a teenager. You had to peer closely, under the pretext of examining pineapples together, to see a faint crosshatching under the eyes. But there was no gray in the cropped hair, and the body in jeans and tee was that of a stripling.

She chose a final avocado. "I am glad to have run into you," she said with her usual courtesy. Even later I could not call this remark valedictory. The Maguires were always glad to run into any of us. They were probably glad to see our backs, too.

"You are a maiden lady," the school doctor reminded me some months later. We have grown old together; he says what he pleases. "Marriage is a private mystery. I'm told that parents feel vacant when their children have flown."

"Most couples just stay here and crumble together."

"Who knows?" he shrugged. "I'm a maiden lady myself."

The few people who saw Keith and Mitsuko waiting for the trolley that September morning assumed they were going off on a camping trip. Certainly they were properly outfitted, each wearing a hiker's back frame fitted with a sleeping bag and a knapsack.

The most popular theory is that they have settled in some other part of the country. There they work—Keith with steel and flame, Mitsuko with the electronic will-o'-the-wisp; there they drink avocado shakes and read paperbacks.

Some fanciful townspeople whisper a different opinion: that when the Maguires shook our dust from their hiking boots they shed their years, too. They have indeed started again elsewhere; but rejuvenated, restored. Mitsuko's little breasts are already swelling in preparation for the expected baby.

I reject both theories. Maiden lady that I am, I believe solitude to be not only the unavoidable human condition but also the sensible human preference. Keith and Mitsuko took the trolley together, yes. But I think that downtown they enacted an affectionate though rather formal parting in some public place—the bus depot, probably. Keith then strode off.

51

Mitsuko waited for her bus. When it came she boarded it deftly despite the aluminum and canvas equipment on her back. The sneakers—bright red, this time, as if they had ripened—swung like cherries from the frame.

The
Large
Lady

Whenever the Foxes give a party, people eagerly come. In the Foxes' big, messy house people feel good. Marty Fox has a born-in-California ease; and Judy's uncorrected Brooklyn accent, here in New England, seems as warm as pastrami. They are attentive hosts, just as they are attentive parents. (Their three sons nevertheless cause them some worry.)

"People with gratifying children," Marlene Winokaur observes on the Friday night of the Foxes' party, "arouse the wrath of their friends."

"Mmm," says her husband, Paul, radiologist and colleague of Marty Fox. And then: "Really?"

In another part of town Frances Masmanian, Judy Fox's co-worker at the Social Service Clinic, is writing down their destination for the sitter.

"Let me ask you a question," says Bill Masmanian. "Why are the Foxes putting themselves to so much trouble?"

"Is it trouble?"

"I was hoping to stay home tonight and grade exams."

"You'll do that tomorrow," says Frances, turning on him the mild, slightly walleyed stare that he loves, or, at least, remembers having loved. So he does not remind her that tomorrow they are going to a Little League game and tomorrow night to a faculty cocktail party and Sunday to a neighborhood meeting. Life in the town of Godolphin, Massachusetts, is chockablock with activity, Bill thinks ungratefully; but how could it be otherwise in a place where so many interesting people choose to live?

Meanwhile, the Foxes were searching their kitchen for stray coffee cups. That this was not an ordinary party—that it was more than social in purpose—had not altered their simple preparations. Marty had bought the wine on his way home from the hospital. He had set up a table for it in the den, where their two older sons would preside. Judy, who didn't work Friday afternoons anyway, had taken on a number of tasks: picking up the platter of turkey and cheese from the deli, spreading a Guatemalan cloth on the big oak table, setting out plates and silverware on the buffet, supplying a McDonald's supper for the boys, and making sure that the bathrooms looked respectable, or at least not repulsive. Today Judy had had the further assignment of pushing the living room chairs against the wall and then setting up twenty-five rented bridge chairs in close rows. All of this work she did unresentfully, her mind busy with one of her clients, a woman whose depression Judy would have liked to relieve. But the woman, mourning a wasted youth, was as yet inaccessible ... Judy had unfolded chairs and swabbed toilets and answered the telephone and thought about her client; and she would have accomplished everything well ahead of time had she not encountered such terrible traffic on her way to and from the airport.

And so, at six-thirty, she was feeling rushed. "All so unnecessary," she complained to Marty. "Mrs. Fenton told me, while we were stuck in the airport tunnel, that she never expected to be picked up at all, that the Organization always pays for a cab. Why couldn't she have said that on the telephone last night?"

"She was too pickled," said Marty. "Which reminds me . . ."

"I bought three jars."

"Kosher spears?"

"Yes. You wondered how I'd recognize the lady, remember? Wait till you see her; you'll know why I didn't have any trouble. She's as big as a house—what crusader against famine wouldn't be?—and as red as a beet. Gray hair scraped into a bun. Glasses, of course, like all the best people"—her own spectacles twinkled— "and an aroma of, uh, recent refreshment."

"Mouthwash?"

Judy nodded. "Preceded by bourbon. She seems eager and clumsy and . . . kind. She was kind to Ricky, who came with me. She and Ricky counted all the No Nukes bumper stickers."

"Did you bring up the movie screen from the basement?"

"Yes, but not the slide projector. She's wearing a navy blue suit. Big shoulders, shiny skirt. She looks like a visiting nurse."

"Are you kidding? Visiting nurses these days are snappy little *shickses* with advanced degrees."

Judy smiled, as she was meant to. "You make good use of your two Yiddish words."

Marty smiled back. "I'll get the projector."

About the bourbon Judy was wrong. It was Scotch that Mrs. Fenton braced herself with. Not so very often. A quick one at lunch, another at around three o'clock, a few before dinner, and a good many at bedtime—but the nightcaps didn't count. Neither did the cocktails. Neither did the noontime snort; she drank less at lunch than most businessmen she'd met. It was only the midafternoon pick-me-up that indicated the . . . incipient problem. But it was only incipient; it was incipient only; and if a bottle or two were part of the provisions that she brought to the Compound when it was time for her tour of duty—well, those bottles were just restoratives, rather like the volumes of Whitman that her closest friend dragged along everywhere, or like the Reverend's needlework. Doilies, antimacassars, tablecloths . . . the man of God crocheted everything. His flying fingers, he claimed, enabled his body to keep still and his heart to refrain from . . . not from breaking, he said with a smile: to refrain from showing its heels. Terrible metaphor, carped the Whitman scholar. Walt would have thrown it out.

Lying shoeless on the bed, Mrs. Fenton reviewed the situation. Her black dress, only slightly malodorous under the arms, hung in the closet. The case of slides was safe in one corner of the room. It had been lugged upstairs by young Ricky, who had then wanted to open it and play with its contents. When she had said no, he had given her a winsome, effeminate look. She had said no again, and he had scampered off, thoroughly boyish. *Damn all kids,* she'd groaned.

She would not have anything to drink now. The good people downstairs would provide wine and a light supper after the presentation. She would not write to her daughter nor her grandchildren; that could wait until tomorrow. She would not itemize her expenditures from this fund-raising trip; that could wait until Monday, when the secretary at the New York headquarters might give her a hand. She would not read; she would not think; she would simply lie here peaceably, gazing with a sort of affection at her feet in their snagged stockings. Women in the Compound Hospital often lay like this. Down the lengths of wasted bodies they communed with their own toes.

People started to arrive at seven. Judy and Marty soon regretted their decision not to serve cocktails. The guests moved awkwardly among the rows of bridge chairs. A few collected in the small space between the front row and the movie screen. One woman reached out and scratched the harsh white surface.

"I can't help thinking that movies are *in* the screen," she confessed to a friend.

"Me, too. And music is in the piano."

"French words are in the plume."

"Of your aunt. Murderous thoughts are in the couch of my analyst."

"You are very silly ladies," said Bill Masmanian.

"Women," corrected one of them.

"However," Bill went on, "scholarly ideas really are in the typewriter. They reside there. Sometimes I have a devil of a time teasing them out. Is there anything like a drink around here?"

Only Marlene Winokaur, sole smoker in the crowd, seemed relaxed. "Where's the speaker?" she puffed at Marty.

"I haven't the fuckiest," he told her. He found his wife in the front hall. "When is Mrs. Fenton coming down?"

"I'm to call her when everyone is here," Judy said.

57

Marty greeted another couple. Then it was Judy's turn. The Foxes didn't confer again for another five minutes. By that time everyone had arrived except for the Satterthwaites, who were always late.

Marty said, "You wake her up. I have to review my introduction."

Judy said, "Okay."

But Mrs. Fenton was already on her way down.

It is the rare person who can descend a stairway with grace. Mrs. Fenton, Judy thought, was to be praised just for staying erect. She was wearing a black wool dress of the sort that, thirty years earlier, Judy's mother had dragged out for second-rate luncheons. Flashing from its front was a diamond pin. Her outfit included a pair of scuffed brown sandals.

"Forgive my shoes," Mrs. Fenton said, one hand gripping the banister. "I forgot to pack my good ones."

Judy said brightly, "Heavens!"

Mrs. Fenton's other hand was grasping the handle of the case of slides. Now, trying to steady its weight against her thigh, she lost hold of her burden, and it dropped. The catch, which Ricky must have been fooling around with, flew apart, and the lid opened slightly, and some of the slides spilled down the stairs.

"They're numbered," said Mrs. Fenton consolingly.

Mrs. Fenton watched while the wife in the plain brown tunic retrieved the slides. The husband—now what on earth was the name of these people? Fitzmaurice? No, that had been the Chicago pair. The husband turned from whatever he'd been reading and moved forward to greet her as she reached the bottom stair. Fox? No, they were in Denver. "Good evening, Mrs. Fenton." They shook hands. What had those busy fingers been up to recently, she wondered: which orifices did they confidently enter? Or perhaps this fellow was the pathologist. She had been lodged with so many doctors. Greenglass! she remembered with relief.

"... and after my few words," he was saying, "we'll turn out the lights and let the presentation begin. Is that how you want it?"

"Yes. The pledge cards..."

"Their little table is on the way to the dining room. There are some others in a box near the wine. In *vino caritas.*"

"I hope so." Oh, she was thirsty. She took the slide case from the hands of her hostess and stepped into the living room. Fortunately the projector and her chair were near the entrance.

"Do you want to see how the thing works?"

She couldn't design a cistern or speak much Somali, but she could handle any goddam projector anybody gave her. However, she allowed him to review the mechanism of his toy. Most of the Greenglasses' guests were seated by now, facing the screen, their backs toward her. Some looked over their shoulders to smile a welcome. Then they faced forward again, for the doctor had made his way to the front of the room.

Mrs. Fenton never listened to the introductory remarks. Since they were all derived from the same mimeographed sheet, they were pretty much alike. The excellent work of the Organization with its three Asian and seven African outposts. The continued need for more support, emotional as well as, of course, financial. The career of today's representative, Alice-Mary Fenton, a former schoolteacher who, fifteen years ago, recently widowed, responded to a call for workers. Has served, in no particular order and sometimes simultaneously, as teacher, administrator, nurse, cook, gardener, teletype operator, jeep driver, labor arbitrator, and practitioner of minor surgery. Ripple of laughter. The members of the Organization staff spend some portion of every year back in this country, interviewing recruits and trying to raise money. Mrs. Fenton is on her stateside tour now. Mrs. Fenton. Mrs. Fenton?

The dogsbody rose. Thank you, she said to her host. She looked around for her hostess, nervous brown tunic, mother of Ricky the Wicked. There she was, off to the side, curled up in one of the real chairs, knuckles against sweet cheek. Thank you, said Mrs. Fenton to Judy. A touch of hunger makes the whole world kin, she said. We'll start with the slides, she said. The doctor turned out the lights.

"Distended bellies," began Mrs. Fenton, "reside on every coffee table." Marlene Winokaur caught the allusion just as Mrs. Fenton, having swallowed, began her second sentence. "I speak of course of *Life,* the *New York Times Magazine.* Magazine Section," she clarified. "And other periodicals, and television. The media, which should excite our sympathies, in fact benumb them. But here is Digo's belly." The voice was neutral, thought Marlene. No, not neutral: unforceful. A slight hoarseness . . . "Digo is six. It never fails to amaze me that not eating can make you fat. He came to the Compound the day before this picture was taken. Here is a slide of him some weeks later," and sure enough, the child's proportions had improved. "Not all of our stories have happy endings, but this one did."

"You have seen pictures like this before." A mass of starving children. "They look pregnant, don't they? But malnutrition comes in other forms." The woman crouching on the straw mat was shapeless because of her wadded garments, but the infant in her arms was all bones. "Paolo could not be saved. Here is Luonne. About thirteen. Anorexic, but not from nerves. The people of

Luonne's tribe subsist on rice and bananas. During famines they try to eat roots and leaves. I have seen, in the operating room, a child whose esophagus had been perforated by the twigs she attempted to swallow, she was so desperate, so willing to die."

Mrs. Fenton paused. Why did she allow herself to relive that moment? Herself holding the retractor, ready to faint, and the nurse turning white above her mask. Later, cradling the little girl in her arms. Mrs. Fenton had wished that the child could have looked last upon a prettier face than her own. What sentiment: the eyes had been blind with dying.

She clicked the slides. Three sentences per slide was a satisfactory tempo, but sometimes she speeded things up. "There are two diseases commonly associated with starvation." Gassem, lying on his cot. "In marasmus, the torso swells while the limbs waste." Reynante, hooked to an IV. "In kwashiorkor, the body develops open sores. Children impassively allow flies to land on their sores." Tiny Asha, who in fact had recovered and been sent home, permanently dulled, on the back of her father. "The parents of these afflicted children, though familiar with death and in particular with infant mortality, still feel, much as we would, that they are letting their offspring down." Frances Masmanian's eyes were hot. "But of course it is we who are letting them down, we whose overconsumption is malnourishing the world. Did you know that the average North American consumes five times as much grain as the average third-world person, much of it in the form of meat, chicken, and eggs? That we foolishly nourish our cattle on this useful grain instead of on greenstuffs that humans can't eat anyway? When I see red meat on the tables of Americans, I want to puke." She wouldn't puke much around here, thought Marty; he and Judy got high on soybeans and fish. "Of course, people avoid the more wasteful foods when they give parties for the Organization." Judy, who served the same delicatessen fare to everybody, even Marty's chief, nevertheless bowed her head. "Of the two," said Mrs. Fenton, showing a hideous picture of a pair of adult sufferers, "marasmus is the more heart-rending, kwashiorkor the more repellent. It is hard not to shudder,"—the suggestible Marlene shuddered—"but whether we shudder in compassion or disgust is difficult to tell. I myself am continually disgusted," she said with momentary agitation. "Here's our refectory," she said more calmly. "That's my best friend in the pith helmet," she said, glad that the show was nearly over, aware that, once again, she had been on the road too long.

Judy's sympathy shifted from the victims, who were pictures, to Mrs. Fenton, who was suffering right here in their house. Perhaps later that evening she would invite Mrs. Fenton into the little sewing room. The children always felt soothed there. Mrs. Fenton could talk—her looseness would be appropriate, even helpful, when they were alone together—and Judy would listen, listen . . . Now all she could do was help her guest bring the presentation to an end.

"We have been criticized for speaking so much about the worst." The front door slammed. The Satterthwaites, elaborately tiptoeing, hung up their own coats. "And indeed at the Compound where I work there is much that is serene, even happy." A rapid succession of slides: women wearing bright garments, children playing games in the mud. "The staff isn't a band of angels by any means. And the victims of misfortune are not better than other people. Our patients can be sly, malicious, ungrateful. Often they smell." Often I hate them. "Also they can be merry." Also I hate you. She pushed irritably at a jammed slide. The screen revealed its next-to-last picture: the Reverend and his patients' chorus. "But we must speak more of the worst than of the good, because otherwise it is impossible, impossible," and here her already harsh monotone became yet more harsh, "to move people to give us money. I have come to ask for contributions, as you know. If I could," she rasped, "I would turn you all upside down and shake you until bank books came out of your mouths. For you are, you know, greedy, selfish, and unChristian." Judy wondered whether now was the moment to intervene. "Just as I am." Marty was sorry the bourbon was in the other room. A snort might calm the lady down. "I too am sinful. I am large; I embrace multitudes. I would not try to induce guilt." Damn right, thought Paul Winokaur, who every day retarded the spread of cancer in numerous patients. "I am begging." Marlene Winokaur felt herself blush.

A long pause. Then Mrs. Fenton's voice continued. "Before we rise to enjoy the Greenglasses' repast, here is the final slide. This boy was perhaps three."

He was crying. Because he was crying, his lids were lowered, and the usual compelling sight of a pair of large eyes was denied to the viewers. His head was bald. Probably shaved, thought Marty Fox. He thought of the parasites that infest the scalp, and then he thought of the ones that make their home in the organs: the trematodes, the nematodes... The small boy's open, unhappy mouth could have been any youngster's mouth, or, at least, any black youngster's; despite malnourishment, the lips retained their Negroid fullness. Marty took note of that. But it was not so much the desolate expression that made the child an effective emblem of deprivation (his picture had already been chosen by the Organization for next year's poster) but his arms. Oh the sticks. Marty kept examining them. The room was silent. God had not meant arms to attain such a disarticulated state. The joints were still sizeable, though. Marty was reminded of a tinkertoy. The fists...the fists pressed against the temples. You could feel the despair. The child's knuckles touched his forehead. It was a universal gesture. Thus have old men grieved for their ruined houses of worship, their conquered cities. Thus grieved the little *schwartse*, for his life.

Judy thought: we are not so bad. But Marlene thought: we are wrong, wrong. Paul Winokaur endured a moment of panic when he couldn't find his wife's tousle of hair, but then he saw it, all filaments, against the whitening walls (Marty Greenglass née Fox was turning on the lights). At that moment, Marty could have renounced the world. Frances Masmanian did resolve to do just that. And though with time their passion weakened and their resolutions faded, they never forgot their feelings on seeing the little boy, nor were their contributions to a variety of relief associations ever less than generous.

The pledges to the Organization that night were large, and the conversations during sandwiches and wine subdued. One woman—the woman who had scratched the movie screen in order to liberate the image within—was unable to talk or eat at all, even when she saw Mrs. Fenton tucking into a turkey-and-Russian. Bill Masmanian agreed with the man who, indicating Mrs. Fenton with his thumb, remarked that lofty ends may rely on low instruments. It was, after all, an old truth.

The Large Lady

A newer truth did occur to Bill. It had to do with all these kindly and generous friends of his, who did not conspicuously consume, who did wonder about the nature of the good life, who gave time and money, feelingly. Hell gapes for the merely empathic: that was what Bill was beginning to think. But since there was no typewriter handy to release its opinions on the matter, Bill lost hold of the idea before the evening was out.

Trifle

Pinky was making the trifle this week. Trifle was the only dessert offered on Thursday nights. It was expected, smiled at, disregarded. The meal itself drew customers to The Local—the soup, the salad, the main dish, the cheese, the wines. And then, at the end of the repast, patrons idly consumed a bit of trifle with their coffee—"real coffee," Marvin called it.

About the trifle, Marvin said to Pinky during her first week at The Local, five months ago—well, he stocked the best rum, the freshest eggs, the thickest cream, and homemade jam. He allowed cakes to dry out. But the trifle remained not quite loved. "Like an orphan," Marvin said.

Pinky looked up from scrubbing a pot. Could he be alluding to her? But no, he was pressing his thumbs onto the cake, assessing its degree of staleness.

Anyway, Pinky wasn't really an orphan. She was a half-orphan at most, and she couldn't be sure even of that. Her father's name was unknown, but that didn't make him dead. He was a number on a folder and some recorded attributes. Caucasian, five feet eleven, without inherited defects. Free of disease, at least on the morning he had donated his sperm. But who knew, maybe he had picked up some slow organism the very next day. Maybe he was dying in agony right this minute; and she, his daughter, was not at his bedside, did not even guess that he was gasping for air. He had been twenty at the time of the donation, a graduate student in Physics. Perhaps he was still a graduate student—he'd be thirty-eight now, they often haunted their departments for decades, doing lab chores and growing wispy beards. She'd seen them at coffee shops near her old home in Providence, Rhode Island.

But maybe Jerkoff had earned his degree after all. Maybe he was working in a lab close to her present home in Godolphin, Massachusetts. Godolphin called itself a Town but was really a leafy wedge of Boston. One noontime he'd walk into The Local in search of an omelet. Or he'd hear of Thursday Nights when the daytime bar and café morphed into a Restaurant. He'd make a reservation; and he'd come in, a little late; and Pinky would serve him, and someone would note the resemblance, and . . . But he was tall, at least according to the form he'd filled out. So why was she was only average? Had he lied about his height?

That was her father—a sociopath.

Her mother? Both of her mothers? A pair of lanky opinions.

One of them, Paula Pinkerton, was a pharmacologist. The other, Mary Kelly, provider of the womb, was a pediatric nurse.

Trifle

Pinky had abandoned them the day she turned seventeen. She didn't go far; Godolphin was only fifty miles from Providence.

I want to live where nobody knows me [she wrote]. You've got to understand. I don't hate you. My post office box is 105446. Don't come after me. I'll write every week. I don't hate you.

We wouldn't dream of coming after you [they wrote back]. Self-actualization is our watchword. We'll send refills of your Ritalin to the post office.

Pinky had stopped taking Ritalin a year ago. Coffee worked much better. For a while she had sold the pills in downtown Providence; later she simply flushed them down the toilet.

In Godolphin she checked into the Y.

She found The Local five days later.

On that warm October day the glass doors had been detached from the central post and folded back into two gleaming accordions. The brass tables were square and the small bar curved. She examined the menu—sandwiches, salads, omelets.

At eleven in the morning there were three patrons, alone, each chewing behind a newspaper.

Pinky leaned against the post.

A man with an abundant mustache—graying blonde, like tarnished gold—was putting condiments and napkin holders on unoccupied tables. He retied his white apron and began to sweep the floor. He nodded at Pinky without speaking. The door into the kitchen was open; no, not open, there wasn't a door at all, just an archway. Pinky saw a sizeable shoulder in a white tee.

She had already been turned down by a dozen nondescript restaurants who didn't need anyone at the moment thanks leave your name. She had conquered her distaste and marched into the Women's Bookstore and Café. "Too late, the position's filled," sighed the proprietor. She had failed to find employment in an organic Undermarket. ("As opposed to Super," the manager explained.) She'd been snubbed by a Cigar Bar downtown. "Too young," the interviewer said, but too chunky was what he meant: face too round, and those eyebrows like awnings...

The man with the mustache was still sweeping.

In the kitchen the shoulder moved again; then a buzz cut came into view over a heavy Asian face; then the whole organism disappeared.

"Can I help you?" said the man with the mustache at last.

Pinky swallowed. "You can give me a job."

He looked at her kindly. "We are four people—Inez and I and Kazuki the Chef and Fogg the Bartender. Those titles are mainly for tax forms. Everybody does a bit of everything. Four is sufficient for our enterprise." After this long-winded refusal he leaned on his broom. "What do you cook?"

"I wasn't aiming to cook, really. Washing up, waitressing, busboy stuff, that's all. Though I do know how to mix a lot of drinks."

"And what do you know how to cook?" he persisted.

"Okroshka, radish pie," she said fast. "Eels, lots of ways." She thought with sudden dismay of the oven at home; its door probably hadn't been opened since her departure. Half-empty Chinese cartons stood on the counter... "Tomato baked with maple," she resumed. "It is an unusual dessert."

"Our dessert is trifle. We make the jam ourselves."

"I've made jam."

But he was no longer listening to her. "The trifle is necessary but incidental."

She attended silently.

"We used to be five," he said.

Pinky inhaled.

"We could be five again."

She held her beath.

"What's okroshka?"

She exhaled. "It's a Russian soup. The recipe calls for cooked chicken, mustard, fresh dill, fresh or dried thyme, and Kvass. Did I mention cucumbers? I usually substitute sour cream and white wine and a little stock for the Kvass. The recipe also calls for pickles, but I only put them in when it's just we three eating. Guests tend to pucker."

"How old are you?"

"Seventeen. Do you want to see my birth certificate?"

"No. Where do you get your eels?"

She told him about the eel ranch in Rhode Island. He was interested also in her apricot chicken and her okra with figs. "Mostly, though," he warned, "you will serve and wash up, just as you offered. Okroshka—a witty name whatever it means."

"It means hodgepodge."

He smiled. "And your own name?"

"Pinkerton Kelly. I'm called Pinky."

They shook hands. "Marvin Fiore. I'm called Marvin. And this"—he extended his hand toward the sidewalk—"is Inez."

———

Inez entered with assumed shyness—for who knew, she said to Pinky later; Pinky might have been a representative of the Health Department in schoolgirl drag. In that case Inez would have managed to sidle into the kitchen and, once there, raise the trap door and clamber down the metal stairs into the basement and sweep away the mouse droppings. "Of course we have mice," she laughed. "Our beloved comensils." Her laugh erased the scar on her chin. When she wasn't laughing the scar looked like a curve drawn deliberately to emphasize the chin's perfection. Pinky looked and looked away; she'd been taught not to goggle at people's unconcealable flaws or at their unconcealable loveliness.

Inez carried a basket of leeks. Her eyes were pennies. Dark curls were silvered here and there. Only the scar interfered with her careless beauty; the scar and also the crooked upper teeth, too many of them, forced to slant backwards into the mouth. The large straight canines looked like fence posts. But her smile was warm despite the unruliness within, or maybe because of it.

"This is Pinky," said Marvin. "Our new associate."

The trifle didn't require the oven. It did require the whole of the supplemental refrigerator, a box the height of a bedside table, the kind of thing that college kids used for beer. This refrigerator had been bought especially for the trifle, though it was home also to Kazuki's insulin and the breast milk for Fogg's infant child. Fogg had to bring the baby to work whenever his wife, a hospital chaplain, was on call. Sometimes this happened on a Thursday night. The child had a name, but everybody followed Marvin's example and called him Blessed Event. Blessed Event usually slept placidly in a wicker basket underneath the bar, but sometimes he did wake up; then someone would plunge the bottle into a cup of very hot water, and then whoever was least in demand would feed the little fellow—Fogg himself, or Marvin, or Inez, or Pinky, or Kazuki; occasionally a trusted guest took on the job.

The trifle was made in two stainless twenty-portion pans. Now Pinky put them side by side on the wooden trestle table. She pressed cake into the bottom of the pans. She poured on rum. She opened the glass preserving jar. The purple jam shivered.

Trout—forty of them currently occupied a wooden ice chest— patiently awaited Kazuki's attention. Tomatoes, now in a basket, would soon offer their smooth cheeks to Inez's knife... "Know what I think?" Pinky said to Marvin, who had put on his quilted vest and taken chopping board and onions onto the back porch to avoid scenting the trifle.

"What do you think?" he amiably asked.

"I think God created potatoes on behalf of our *Patate in Tegame*." She spread jam on top of the soaked cake.

"You are a sentimental goose," he replied. "Goose, goose—shall we do a goose one of these days?"

"Oh, Lord, yes, with prune dressing." Her mind skidded helplessly back to the Christmas before last; meanwhile she dropped custard onto the layer of jam, spoonful by spoonful. Her mothers had given a holiday party for twenty people. She had roasted a goose. "You have a rare talent," said one of the guests, rising from the crowded table and lifting his glass, his dyed hair greenish under the cruel light of the chandelier. "Pinky we love you," and he probably did, they probably all did, those couples, some tender, some uneasy, some disappointed... She was still covering jam with custard. "My parents are *embarazo grande*," her

73

best eighth-grade friend Evangelista had once confessed. "Five years in this country, maybe fifty words of English. Yet they're *muy* intelligent," she added fiercely, as if Pinky might suggest otherwise.

"The custard is depleted," said Marvin. "You are spooning air."

Pinky stored the two pans of trifle in the little refrigerator. This past Christmas she had feasted with Marvin and Inez and the others in their narrow brick house just on the border of Boston. On holidays and Sundays the staff always gathered for supper at the Fiores'. Attendance seemed to be one of the terms of employment.

On Sundays Kazuki brought his ancient mother. On Sundays cheerful, freckled Fogg brought his cheerful, freckled wife, who always wore a turtleneck as if it approximated a priest's collar; or maybe she too bore a scar, located, unlike Inez's, in a place of concealment. She carried Blessed Event. Inez cooked a new dish—a thick soup, maybe, or a ragout, testing it out; and they all dined together at a round table, shoulder to shoulder, an experience impossible at the busy Local; and Marvin toasted Our Family; and the dark unused bedrooms upstairs weighed on Pinky's spirits which were never high on Sundays anyway—for what were they doing back in Providence without Pinky to interpret the news to, or to drag along to a dreary art film, or to hold the sign at a demonstration while they shouted: the two of them in similar but not identical long ash-colored coats and cropped pewter hair; really, home with its pale walls and engravings and vases of eucalyptus was composed of hundreds of shades of gray.

"I already told you: I don't know why they never had children," Kazuki had snapped. "I suppose you're always asking *them* why I never got married." No, she wasn't. She'd met plenty of Kazukis, comfortable solitaries, not yearning after men, not yearning after women.

"Marvin and I discussed it only once," Fogg told her. "They kept trying, you know, well maybe you don't, anyway it got too late and not everyone wants to go to Romania, who can tell what you'd come back with; and not everyone wants to hire a surrogate or have a blind date with a sperm bank." She'd looked at him sharply; but his expression was innocent. "I think they've adjusted. They like our son." And so Pinky, cold with fear, imagined Inez snatching up Blessed Event one Thursday night, running with him into the black street, leaping onto a trolley, then a train, then a bus, finally crossing the Mexican border... Fogg, not party to this vision, serenely polished wineglasses.

Christmas—two months ago now; turkey stuffed with olives— had turned out to be like Sunday suppers, only longer. There was a tree and there were presents. Marvin and Inez gave Pinky earrings, which she guessed she'd have to wear. Fogg and his wife gave her a book about the South Pole, which she guessed she'd have to read. Kazuki and his mother gave her a framed print of Hokusai's *The Great Wave.* She liked it. Her mothers sent a red bathrobe.

After dinner they sang carols. Kazuki—whose father had been Irish, though no one could tell by looking at him—sang "Mither Machree" in a strong tenor. "I inherited two cuisines," he said. "They cannot be folded into each other," he lamented.

Pinky amused the baby. Marvin beat Fogg's wife at chess. Everybody played poker. Kazuki's mother won three dollars. There was no talk about animal rights, same sex marriage, the National Endowment for the Arts, or the work of Djuna Barnes.

75

Now Pinky turned her attention to odd jobs—grating horseradish for the salad dressing, slicing potatoes for the *Patate,* trundling the barrow over to the cleaners to pick up the white tablecloths that were used only on Thursdays. She had to wait while a guy who looked like Albert Einstein left an old tweed suit to be cleaned. The thing was shredding. He was an absent-minded physicist, for sure—but too old, and much too short.

Then it was six o'clock. She went upstairs to put on her waitress's black dress and her earrings.

The room and bathroom over the kitchen had been scrubbed and painted before she moved in. Striped curtains beautified the single window—curtains run up by Inez on one of the gloomy days when she stayed home. On the floor lay a woven rug Fogg found in a yard sale. *The Great Wave* hung over the bed.

Among the new things Pinky had discovered two pieces of old evidence.

One was a vial of pills lying on its side in a back corner of a bookshelf. The vial was dusty, its label long since curled off; and the pills were various shapes and sizes and pastel tints; and some were capsules, the slow-acting enteric kinds; and some were little half-ovals, sliced by a razor.

The other item was a photograph, stuck behind the middle drawer of the bureau. Three people smiled from the snapshot: Inez and Marvin, about ten years earlier, and an unidentified young man. His gold-rimmed glasses reflected light away from eyes and eyebrows. His hairline receded gently. His lips were drawn back into a sad smile.

Not hard to figure out who he was. He was Marvin's business

partner. He was Inez's lover. He had turned a knife against Inez when she refused to leave Marvin for him. He had been banished.

Where was he now?

How was he faring without his pills?

Patrons began to arrive at seven forty-five, and by a few minutes past the hour almost all the tables were filled. Conversation strummed, laughter twanged. Kazuki stirred the soup and sang "Rose of Tralee" under his breath.

Pinky and Fogg brought tall glasses of champagne to each guest. "My disappointment is profound," Pinky heard an elegant man saying to Inez; and as he spoke he rose on the tips of his polished shoes. "I heard about The Local across the waters, in Paris."

"I am sorry you didn't hear about the need for reservations," Inez said smoothly. "Please come tomorrow for lunch; we may have some trifle left."

He bowed over her fingers.

Most guests were not tourists. Guidebooks ignored The Local— it served dinner only on Thursdays, and it didn't advertise. A recent newspaper review—newspapers did grudgingly pay attention— praised the food and then complained about the lack of choice.

"Choice: what an overvalued commodity," Marvin remarked.

The early arrivals were finishing their champagne cocktails. Later ones were beginning theirs. The very latest were entering. The folding glass doors, now affixed with storm panes, were drawn together. The next-to-last customer entered, a furred woman—and how warm that gleaming longhaired collar looked against the wind-chapped face. Kazuki showed her to a table for one. A table for one was a financial loss, but The Local did not discriminate against isolates. The last foursome came in now, smiling at people here and there; and the door shut for good.

Inez, serving champagne, paused to greet a pair of frequent patrons. Tonight they occupied the best place in the house—the crescent table in the far corner made by glass and wall, a table where two people side by side could observe the bar, and the kitchen, and the other guests. If they turned leftwards they could see the sidewalk glowing under golden street lights, and parked cars crusted with snow.

Pinky cleared the champagne glasses. In the kitchen Kazuki ladled out the soup—puree of kale and broccoli. He put a spoonful of vinegary tomatoes in each bowl. Fogg uncorked bottles at this table, at that. Inez and Pinky served soup. Fogg poured wine. Fogg served soup. Marvin served soup. Inez ladled soup. Kazuki ladled soup. Blessed Event cheeped. Pinky served soup, and then stepped behind the bar. "Not yet," she soothed. The baby smiled.

A murmur of voices. A gentle slurping. The mild clatter of dishes being removed.

A few minutes of repose.

The salad, now, with horseradish dressing.

Forks clinked against plates. Voices caressed voices. Pinky filled the dishwasher. Kazuki slid trays of *Patate* out of the oven and replaced them with trays of trout, which he had butterflied and lightly oiled and sprinkled with his private herb mixture. Inez stirred lemongrass carrots and caramelized onions. Pinky warmed the baby's bottle. The five workers formed an assembly line: Kazuki at trout and *Patate*, Pinky at carrots and onions, Marvin and Inez and Fogg without apparent haste whisking the dishes to the patrons. The final two tables were served only by Marvin and Fogg. Inez, seated on a low stool behind the bar, had taken the now noisy baby in her arms; and only someone standing in the back corner near the restrooms could see her in the bar mirror, crouched over the little thing. Could see her, though not her scar. Could see her, though not her prominent canines.

Pinky unloaded the soup plates from the dishwasher, put in the salad plates.

Kazuki went into the back yard to smoke a narrow cigar.

Fogg glided from table to table, adding wine to wine, mineral water to mineral water.

Marvin stood in the corner near the restrooms, almost invisible. But Pinky in the archway of the kitchen knew what to look for. A metallic curve catching a gleam of light—his mustache. A starched wedge—the shirt under his tuxedo jacket. Four small triangles of pale blue neon—the whites of his eyes. He was watching, through the mirror: the gentle motherly crouch; the chin which had once been slashed; the mouthful of muddled teeth guarded by fangs.

Peace descended upon Pinky—the contentment of the nourisher. The kid she'd been, preparing splashy meals, had never felt such satisfaction, though her skinny mothers tried to be appreciative. But they would have preferred suppers of soy butter and Granny Smiths. When she served okroshka they liked the pickles best. Trifle? They would have gagged.

A newcomer to The Local lit a cigarette.

Marvin moved forward. "I'm sorry—at the bar only."

The stranger took his habit to the bar and sat down. Marvin placed the house ashtray within reach. The smoker could not see Inez and Inez could not see him.

Peace descended upon the customers too. They bent forward toward each other across their messy plates—or, in the case of the woman alone, bent forward toward an invisible companion. They conferred—about business, about art, about the neighbors. Pinky heard the baby's pleased burp, but only because she was listening for it. The smoking customer heard it too—she saw his face turn confusedly toward the kitchen, some funny noise, oh well. He stubbed out his cigarette and returned to his table.

In a seemingly leisurely fashion the five staff members cleared the plates.

A few minutes of repose.

The cheese course now: a bit of Roquefort, a bit of pimentoed chevre. Kazuki was whipping the cream.

Then another wait. How important the space between events, Marvin said.

Kazuki drew the trays of trifle out of the refrigerator. He threw the whipped cream onto the trays as if he were tossing a bucket of suds onto the sidewalk. Despite this offhandedness the cream settled in gentle peaks on one pan and then on the other until each looked like a Hokusai scene. He cut the dessert into squares. Fogg's wife, her shift over, slipped into the kitchen. Inez and Pinky and Fogg served trifle and Marvin went around with his coffeepot. "Yes, caffeinated," he said without apology. And wasn't it amazing, it was always amazing, people drank the caffeinated coffee; and Pinky was sure that within an hour they'd all be asleep like the baby behind the bar, now blissfully snoozing on his mother's shoulder.

———

And she too—she who had needed three hundred milligrams of Trazodone when she was living at home—she too slept eight hours every night, unmedicated.

But tonight she was suddenly awake.

Plonk. Plonk. Rubber against brick; she knew that sound.

She went to her one window and surveyed, like a princess, the porched three-decker houses, and the gabled Victorians, and the few elms remaining: elms far apart enough not to have caught or transmitted the Dutch Disease. Necessary space, Marvin said. Moonlight turned the snow in their back yard into satin, like a wedding gown, like the two wedding gowns they wore the day they got married, she Pinky then four, the flower girl ... And there, standing in the middle of that oblong of glistening white, his familiar face raised to hers, about to throw the tennis ball again, was the man in the picture.

Plonk.

Their eyes met.

Let me in? he mouthed.

So she did.

"They changed the lock!" he said, throwing his coat deftly at the hook. It landed, it swung ... "Who are you?"

A staff member, she said; his replacement, she supposed; of course he could have his old job back, she quickly added.

"Good Lord, no. I'm doing fine in Philadelphia. The lens business. That food we served gave me reflux. I was always trying new pills."

"Oh."

"I drove up on a whim; but I got here too late to wake up my sister."

"Oh."

"So I thought I'd crash at The Local. But the lock..." He rubbed his thick brows. "Could we have some coffee?"

Pinky warmed the pot and poured coffee into mugs. He got brandy from the bar and laced each mug. She took the last piece of trifle from the refrigerator and cut it in half and put it on two plates on the trestle table. He laid out two forks. They sat opposite each other. His hair had receded further.

"They changed the lock for my sake," Pinky said. "To make me feel secure."

"Oh. Hey, this goo's better than it used to be. Not quite loved, a foundling... Isn't that how he says it?"

"Pretty much."

"How does she seem?"

Pinky considered. "Melancholy some of the time. Resigned the rest of the time. Happy on Thursdays." She sipped, took courage. "I saw you in a photograph—I thought you were her...paramour."

"Hell, no, just the kid brother."

"And her chin—it wasn't you who cut it up?"

"Inez did that herself—no, don't look like that, it was an accident with a grapefruit knife."

"I figured you'd been exiled."

"Dramatic, aren't you. I walked out to live my own life. Our mother and father are dead. But Marvin and Inez kept acting like parents... Any more trifle?"

"No. How did Marvin and Inez act like parents? My mothers, they mostly march for causes and otherwise sit in armchairs..."

"They wanted me to tell them everything I did and thought. Hey. How many mothers have you got?"

"... in armchairs, talking." Hardworking women, growing old. How jolly the red of this bathrobe. Her eyes stung.

There was a long silence; a peaceful lag.

"Two," Pinky heard someone say. "I have two mothers." Was that voice hers? "I had a father too, but none of us met him. He was necessary but incidental. Would you like to borrow my sleeping bag?"

"I'll spread it out behind the bar," he said.

It was a month later. Kazuki had made the trifle this week. Pinky had made the okroshka. As always the reservation list was full. The meal was venison braised with raspberries. Fogg's brother had shot the deer.

Patrons were entering. One couple arrived on a motorcycle. A cab brought four others. The pair Pinky was watching for was coming by car. They were a little late. That would be Mary's doing—fussing about locks, about lights, while Paula stood at the door of the house twirling her keys and whistling. But they were not very late. Pinky was opening a bottle of champagne when she saw them come in. Marvin ushered them to the crescent table. Inez poured mineral water and bestowed her generous smile. In the kitchen archway, Kazuki bowed. Fogg's hand rested briefly on Pinky's shoulder. "Easy does it," he said.

Carrying two golden glasses, Pinky walked forward to greet her parents.

Vegetarian Chili

T o the Editor of *Cuisine:*

Donna's Ladle is charmed to be asked to contribute a recipe to your forthcoming issue "Crowd Pleasing." We are not *exactly* a restaurant; but we can certainly use your guest chef's fee of $250 to buy shopping carts and bras for our own guests and a sparker to light the burners on the stove. Josie's eyebrows are only now growing back.

To prepare vegetarian chili I soak beans the night before. The next morning, after opening the church basement door, yelling at the mice, turning on the stove, and welcoming the patrons who have huddled all night on the portico, I start cooking the beans. Then I follow these directions:

Sort donated vegetables. Reject those too moldy to be identified. Chop. Do not let Maryanne near knives.

Heat oil in pans; sauté veggies. Persuade Akisha's children not

85

to drown dolls in caldrons. Sit with Bridget, crying over the baby who died. Mix eggs, cornmeal and milk in likely ratio and set in oven. Do something about Gretel's raw feet. Combine veggies, beans, tomato juice, chili powder. Skimpy? Extend with yesterday's meatloaf; it's mostly vegetables, to tell the truth.

Chili and cornbread will serve seventy-five generously, fifty very generously. Usually serves 100, who are more or less pleased.

Sincerely,
Donna Crowninshield, Chef

Rules

One autumn Donna's Ladle—a soup kitchen for women operating out of the basement of Godolphin Unitarian Church— became all at once everybody's favorite cause. "There are fashions in charity just as in bedslippers," sniffed Josie, who had been working as a volunteer since the Ladle's beginning six years earlier. "Don't count on this popularity to last, Donna."

Donna never counted on anything to last. But she was grateful for the new help. A group from a local synagogue undertook to deliver cooked delicacies. The members of the Godolphin Helping Hands raked each other's closets for clothing contributions. Maeve, a nearby Catholic Women's College, posted the Ladle's flier on its bulletin board. As a result, a few eager students appeared almost every day. Some needed firsthand material for term papers on poverty. The others showed up out of simple good-heartedness.

"Mother Theresas in designer jeans," said Josie privately to Donna. But to the Maeve students Josie was a model of patience, repairing the Cuisinart whenever they broke it, and demonstrating a restrained kindness toward the guests that the girls meant to emulate, really they did. They just couldn't help overreacting to the tragic tales they heard. They were frequently in tears. Their eyes, even when red with weeping, were large and lovely.

"Those kids are prettier at that age than I ever thought of being," Donna remarked at a staff meeting. "Is it their faith?"

Beth said, "It's their smiles. All those buckteeth bursting out at you." And she smiled her own small sweet crescent. "Orthodontia can be a cruel mistake."

Pam went further, grinning like a schoolboy. "Orthodontia is child abuse."

Her colleagues laughed at this distortion. They were not caseworkers, not sociologists, not child advocates—they were just the staff of the Ladle, three overworked young women—but they had seen children who had been abused. They had broken bread with the abusers. They had witnessed—and put a stop to—beatings by enraged mothers. "You can't hit anybody here," they each knew how to say in a voice both authoritative and uncensuring. A few weeks ago, Pam, turning white with fury hours after the event, reported to the others that she had interrupted Concepta peppering her grandson, a niño of eighteen months.

"Peppering him?" asked Donna. "Peppering him with what?"

"Peppering him with pepper. She had him on her lap and she was shaking the pepper jar over him as if he were a pizza. I don't think any got into his eyes. But I wanted to strangle the bitch." Pam bit her lip and bent her curly head.

"What happened next?" Donna mildly inquired.

"I said, 'Please stop that, Concepta. You can't hurt people here.'

And I sat down beside her and she handed the kid over with a giggle. 'We were only having fun,' she told me. I dandled him and he stopped crying and after a while I handed him back. What else could I do?"

"Not a thing," said Beth softly, her plump little hands stirring in her lap.

"Not a damned thing," said Donna.

Reporting incidents to the authorities was out of the question. Donna's Ladle rarely knew the last names of its guests, nor even their real first names if they chose to glide in under a *nom de guerre*. Their addresses, if they had any, were their own business. This peppering was thus far an isolated event. Concepta usually came in alone, drunk but not drinking. ("You can't drink here" was another rule. Shouting and doping were also forbidden. All four rules were frequently broken.)

"Did you suggest the Children's Room?" Donna asked Pam.

Pam lifted her narrow shoulders. "I'd suggested that earlier, before she decided to season him. But Concepta didn't want her niño anywhere near Ricky Mendozo, and Ricky was in the Children's Room that morning. 'Might catch it,' Concepta said."

Ricky Mendozo's mother had AIDS. Ricky himself was a sickly child, often hospitalized. Donna and Pam and Beth understood Concepta's reluctance to let her grandchild play with the runny-nosed, frequently soiled Ricky. As far as the staff knew Ricky did not have AIDS. But the staff didn't know very much.

Some things they did know. They knew that the little kids who came in liked stuffed animals and trucks and toys you could ride and toys you could climb into. They liked crayons and paint. They didn't like to put things away. They liked to hurl things around; and

89

to hurl themselves around; and to sit on laps. They enjoyed ice cream, though they were fearful of getting themselves dirty. They were loud and possessive and self-centered; but they had learned somewhere that when you grabbed a toy from another child you had to shout "Share!"

But when their mothers or aunts or grandmothers or father's girlfriends retrieved them after lunch, something frightened could be felt to uncoil within certain of these stained, smelly little persons. The children did their part in the rough ceremony of reunion—"Where the fuck's your cap?" "Did you make a mess like always?"—by producing an article of clothing or feinting at mopping some milk. But the staff felt their hearts sink, and the Maeves claimed that theirs broke in two, at the premonition of outrage that might follow, back in the welfare motel, or the scabby apartment, or the room grudgingly loaned by a sister-in-law, places where even the bare-bones rules of Donna's Ladle did not prevail. "He had such a nice morning," shuddered a Maeve one mild November afternoon, as the voice of Nathaniel's mother shot through an open basement window from the sidewalk: "You do what I say, hear? Or else!"

"'Or else' may mean no more than a slap," said Donna to the worried girl. "And he did have a nice morning. That's important."

It was important to keep the Children's Room open, even though maintaining the play area meant that there were fewer hands making lunch in the kitchen. Some children had become regulars—Nathaniel, Cassandra, Africa, Elijah. Others visited from time to time. These days—because of the Helping Hands' clothing drive—the Ladle's youngest guests wore outfits that had originated in Neiman-Marcus and Bloomingdale's.

But the erect and solemn girl of about seven who appeared one December morning was not wearing the castoffs of a Godolphin child—not of a twentieth-century child, anyway. Her long dress of gray flannel might have belonged to an early citizen of Massachusetts Bay if it had not had a back zipper. The woman who accompanied the child was garbed also in a long plain home-sewn dress. They wore identical brown capes. Each had a single braid, thick and fair. The child's straight-browed gray eyes resembled her mother's. But the girl lacked the scar that ran down the left side of the woman's face from the lower lid to the middle of the cheek.

When they arrived Beth was circulating through the large basement dining-room with a tray of knishes. "Hello," she said. "I'm Beth."

A silence followed. "Yes," said the woman at last.

At Donna's Ladle the staff restricted its questions to matters of food and comfort. And so: "Would you like a meat pastry?" said Beth, bending down to the child. "Take two." But the child, with murmured thanks, took only one.

Beth straightened up. "We're glad to have you with us," she said. "Please feel at home. We serve lunch at noon. Sit at any table. Breakfast fixings are on the buffet against the wall. The Quiet Room is behind you," and she pointed with her free hand. "The Children's Room is next to it." She backed away. "Feel at home," she repeated weakly, realizing that this couple would not feel at home anywhere.

Beth reported her encounter to Donna, who was concocting a sweet-and-sour sauce in the kitchen. Donna handed the wooden spoon to a volunteer and moved to the pass-through, from which vantage point she could see the entire dining room.

"On the right," said Beth.

91

Donna was distracted by the sight of twenty-year-old Bitsy crooning to a stuffed animal. "Off her meds?"

"Yes. Says they addle her."

Donna shifted her gaze to the next table. She saw the new guests. They were seated side by side. The child's hands, clasped, rested on the table. The mother's hands lay in her lap. Each was attentive to the space in front of her eyes . . . to the vision of some New Jerusalem, Donna suspected.

"Adventuresses, do you think?" said Beth. "I'll go have a chat with poor Bitsy."

"Actresses on their lunch break," suggested Pam, at Donna's other shoulder. "What's that Arthur Miller play?"

"*The Crucible*," said Donna. Pam moved off.

"They're like from another world," breathed a Maeve who had replaced Beth.

And Josie had replaced Pam. "Weirdos."

Donna didn't reply. These newcomers were not the poor she had always with her. She was used to cheats and crazies, drunks and dealers. She was fond of little retired chambermaids whose voices still shivered with brogues; they relied on the Ladle to augment their pitiful pensions. She liked hot-tempered sisters from the South and the South Bronx; she viewed with puzzled respect magic-mongers from the Islands; and she was even accustomed to certain outspoken religious zealots—Shrews of Christ, Josie called them. But plain-living Puritans—what were they doing in her facility?

The pair didn't look needy. But the Ladle's policy must hold: no prying. Among the guests were a few batty gentlewomen who might well possess million-dollar trust funds, who probably lunched at the Ritz on the days that the Ladle was closed. They were served without question. So too would this mother and daughter be served. It was the rule.

In the months that followed, Donna and Beth and Pam learned a few facts about the mother and daughter, facts which they shared at the weekly staff meetings. The woman's name was Signe. The child's was Rhea. Signe was separated from Rhea's father, a clergyman. Signe and Rhea lived in two basement rooms, just over the line in Boston. They received a monthly check from the clergyman. It met their wants. "But only barely," said Signe to Donna. "We are grateful to the Ladle for our breakfasts and lunches."

"I'm so glad. But there are other sources you could tap, too," Donna responded. "The state government supplements inadequate incomes, and the city itself..."

"No."

After a few minutes Donna said idly, "We sometimes hear of jobs. Tailoring work."

"Rhea is my work."

Donna looked at the severe little girl, who was reading a thick book. The Bible? Donna wondered, craning her neck.

"It was Grimm's," she reported that week. "In the Modern Library edition. No pictures. Impressive."

"Signe teaches her at home," said Beth.

"Isn't that against the law?"

"No," said Pam; and then looked down at her hiking boots. She was terrified of seeming to show off.

"Tell us," Donna laughed.

Pam ran both hands through her curls. "There's a law that even provides for home schooling, sets down regulations. But the person who teaches has to take a test, and a curriculum has to be followed, and materials... Signe would probably meet the requirements." Pam shrugged. "I doubt she's deigned to apply."

Signe and Rhea spent most mornings in the Children's Room. Shortly before lunch they selected places at a table in the dining room. Before they ate they bowed their heads in silent prayer, and then quietly and with perfect manners dispatched whatever was set before them; then they returned to the Room. There Rhea sat on a low chair beside her mother with her book, turning pages, rarely looking up.

A Maeve named Michelle—the fifth of seven children—took a sisterly interest in Rhea. She offered to play with the girl. She offered to walk with her to the park. On one occasion she offered to tell Rhea some Navajo fables. "I'm minoring in Folklore," she confided to the Children's Room at large. "I'm majoring in American Women. I'm writing my senior paper on Donna."

Donna was scraping dried oatmeal from the easel. She raised her eyes. "Don't you dare."

"Oh, it's almost finished," said Michelle.

Michelle's invitations to Rhea were always met with a polite refusal—from the child; the mother listened without comment.

"There's a lovely pulpit upstairs," said Michelle one morning. "Shall we have a look at it together?"

"No, thank you."

"Wouldn't you like to see my dormitory? It's just a few blocks away."

"No, thank you."

Donna had to take Michelle aside. "I think perhaps—if you're just nearby, like an old tree, she'll eventually come to you."

"She's so lonely," wailed Michelle.

"Little Cassandra would love to build a block tower."

"Cassandra's no challenge."

"Yes, well, but," murmured Donna. "Okay?"

When Rhea did play she played by herself: arranged the doll house, or drew elaborate diagrams that looked like plans for lace tablecloths. Meanwhile Signe actually did crochet, her hands and hook converting a ball of wheat-colored thread into a long loose fabric. The ball of thread lay in a canvas sack, and the fabric she made dropped slowly into the sack too, and so none of the staff knew whether Signe was making afghan strips or dresser scarves or just yards of trimmings. The woman was as silent and as absorbed as her daughter. Once in a while, though, when one of the toddlers became difficult, she would put down her crocheting, rise from the chair, and pick up the whining or bawling or flailing child. The child grew instantly quiet, either borrowing Signe's composure or becoming paralyzed with terror. After a few minutes Signe set the youngster down and returned to her work, her scar glistening like the trail of a tear.

The winter wore on. There were two fist fights. There was a fight with knives; the police had to be called. Concepta was caught drinking in the bathroom and was barred for a week. An elderly guest was found dead in her rented room. Another was found almost dead in an alley. Pam began to lead after-lunch discussions on subjects like Self-Esteem and Expectations. Cassandra and her mother stopped coming to the Ladle. Over dessert one afternoon Donna wondered aloud what had become of them. Her table erupted with answers.

"They went South."

"They went to New York."

"The gran took them back."

"She married that sonofabitch."

Donna was impressed by this group confabulation. She lit a rare cigarette. Cassandra and her mother would return. Or else they would not.

"But all those explanations can't be true," said Michelle to Donna as she took away the dishes.

"Sure they can. *Seriatim*. It's not our business, toots."

"Whose business is it?"

"The parole officer's. You've got to take some things as you find them, Michelle."

Michelle wheeled furiously away. She deposited her stack of dishes in the pass-through. Noisily scraping a chair, she sat down beside a guest who had once practiced law. Donna heard the girl enthusiastically propose that the former lawyer write down some of her experiences. The delighted guest understood this as an invitation to dictate her autobiography. "I am born," she began.

Donna considered rescuing her acolyte, thought better of it, took refuge in the Children's Room. Within a few minutes she was sitting cross-legged on the floor. Ricky Mendozo was sniffling in her lap. Nathaniel and Elijah were lining up trucks, squabbling lightly. Bitsy lounged in the doorway, a teddy bear under her arm.

"The sauce on the fish was funny today," said Bitsy. "Did you make it, Donna?"

"Josie made it."

"The volunteer that looks like a parrot?"

"She has red hair and dresses colorfully," Donna sidestepped.

"What's in that sauce, huh?"

"Yoghurt and mayonnaise."

"Where's my Nathaniel!" said Nathaniel's mother, bursting past Bitsy.

"I prefer lemon butter," said Bitsy.

"You, Nathaniel. Ain't you ready?"

Nathaniel ran toward Donna. Ricky, still in Donna's lap, gave him a feeble kick. Nathaniel yelled and punched Ricky. Nathaniel's mother slapped Nathaniel. Elijah threw a truck at Bitsy.

The trouble swirled and then settled. Donna got help from Michelle, who thereby escaped from the lawyer's reminiscences. By three o'clock most of the children and their mothers had been bundled out. Beth and some volunteers were putting the kitchen to rights. Michelle was singing to Africa. Pam was managing to calm Elijah's gorgeous turquoise-eyed mother, who claimed that her social worker had recommended prostitution as a career. Donna was mopping the dining room.

"Good-bye," said a low voice: Signe's. She was carrying her sack and several books. Rhea too had books within each elbow. Their capes, widened by their burdens, looked like bat wings.

Many guests made use of the public library. Free toilets, a choice of periodicals, chairs to snooze in. But Signe and Rhea actually borrowed and returned books. They patronized the museum, too; a volunteer had spotted them at a lecture on Dutch Interiors. And Pam had once seen them at the State House, listening to a debate on the budget. Those events were probably part of Rhea's schooling. They were Fine Arts and Social Studies field trips, just like the ones taken by schoolchildren, but uncomplicated by questions of who would sit next to whom on the bus. Rhea would end up better educated than her cohorts. "She'll get into Harvard," Pam had predicted. "That's more than I did."

But Donna thought that the girl would be better off in a classroom, learning to tolerate and interact and share. Schools weren't meant only for the likeable. There must be a place for this scarily self-possessed miniature of her mother. Let Signe crochet in the corridor if the two couldn't bear separation. Let them practice their queer habits somewhere else.

"Good-bye," Donna said.

She watched them go. She leaned on her mop, letting her distaste for the pair flood her cheeks. The motherly slaps and threats and insults she countenanced every day at the Ladle didn't bother her as much as Signe's austere silence. She wondered if Signe controlled her girl by means of some drug undreamed of by the street-smart clientele of the Ladle—brimstone, maybe, bubbling on the stove in their basement apartment.

"Am I glad them two is gone," Africa's aunt said, finally coming out of the john. She tied Africa's knitted hat so tightly that the child's face bulged beneath it.

"Which two?"

"Which two? The devil and her child. They give me the creeps. And is you the cutest cookie God ever made?" she inquired of Africa, who burbled something in return.

"Isn't the devil a man, Ollie?"

"He can put on a dress, honey. Do you happen to have an extra buck or two? Pampers is so expensive."

Pampers were indeed expensive. They were regularly stolen from stores and resold on the street; the entrepreneurs involved made a tidy supplemental income. Donna gave Ollie both money and pampers; and was rewarded by a mammoth embrace that made her grin—it was so easy, so emphatic, so momentarily sincere, so ultimately meaningless. "Hug me again," demanded Donna.

Ollie complied. Then: "How about another pamper?"

Donna gave her the rest of the box of diapers. Ollie and Africa jounced away. *"You're* the devil," Donna called after them, laughing. As for Signe—she was merely a visitor from a strict, drear world.

Donna turned her thoughts to current problems. The Helping Hands had dropped the Ladle in favor of Animal Rights. The Maeves' attendance had slackened, though Michelle remained faithful. The price of vegetables was going up; even broccoli was almost out of sight. Mice were running free in the pantry. Tomorrow, Thursday, might be a nightmare. Pam was to lead an after-lunch discussion of Empowerment; and who knew what would ensue? Last month the Empowerment session had ended in disarray: the former lawyer had lengthily cited cases; Bitsy in disgust had poured iced tea down a new guest's back. Perhaps tomorrow's meeting would be more orderly. A representative from the Governor's office had promised to drop in. Donna hoped he wouldn't get the iced tea.

In fact, the Empowerment discussion went well. The guests who attended drafted a petition protesting budget cuts. Bitsy caused no trouble: she stayed in the Children's Room with Michelle and Elijah. In the dining room Elijah's mother sat next to the Governor's representative and with judicious obscenity explained exactly how this State had failed her. A knapsack containing all her belongings lay on the table in front of her; she punched it for emphasis. The Governor's representative jotted down some notes, but mostly he stared hungrily at Elijah's beautiful mother—at her glossy hair, braided like an Indian bride's; at her ivory skin; at her long blue-green eyes.

Toward the end of the discussion Donna saw the supermarket's boy trundle in a case of young asparagus, as mauve as a rabbit's nose. "Donation!" he yelled. The pantry mice, she'd noticed, had swallowed all their poison. They must be back behind the walls, dying.

And now it was Friday afternoon. Free Food had just delivered several baskets of very soft tomatoes. The staff would stew them as soon as possible. Pam and Donna were separating the merely overripe from the absolutely rotten.

"I got a glimpse of Signe's handiwork the other day," Pam said. "What's it like?"

"Like nothing I've ever seen. It's a hollow coil that seems to turn inside out every so often. I can't imagine its purpose."

"A noose, maybe?"

Pam shuddered. "She probably rips it out every night, like what's her name."

"Penelope. But Signe does make their clothing. She can do useful needlework."

"Maybe the coil is her hobby," said Pam. "Ugh," she said, as a tomato imploded on her palm.

Most of the guests had left. The staff and the volunteers mopped the floors and cleaned the kitchen and stacked chairs and tables. Michelle, on her way to a weekend with her boyfriend, ran by—a toothy smile, a pair of fast denim legs. "Oh, Donna, I forgot to put away the cleaning bucket in the Children's Room. Have to catch the bus. Sorree!" Donna waved her on and went into the empty Children's Room to fetch the bucket.

But the Children's Room wasn't empty. Signe and Rhea sat on their low chairs, facing each other. They were reciting something in words Donna couldn't catch—a tuneless but emotional song consisting of questions and responses. Signe intoned the questions. Rhea declared the responses. The child's eyes were closed, her sparse lashes long on her unmarked cheeks. Signe's eyes were open, watching the girl with consuming interest. "You can't..." Donna began, lurching forward, banging her shin on Michelle's pail.

Rhea opened her eyes. Both Signe and Rhea turned to look at Donna, who was standing on one leg now, rubbing the other. We can't what? they seemed to be inquiring. What rule were they breaking? They were not drinking. They were not doping. They were not yelling. They were not striking each other. The tone of their liturgy was charged but it wasn't abusive. How was Donna to finish her admonition—you can't look peculiar? You can't try to save your child from corruption? You can't pray?

"Sorry," she muttered. Limping, she pushed the wheeled pail out of the Children's Room. The harsh duet resumed. Rhea's words sounded like numbers. Perhaps she was reciting the populations of the world's capitals. Perhaps she was calculating square roots.

Whatever her catechism, it was soon over. Mother and daughter emerged, now in their capes, while Donna was putting away a stack of newly washed tablecloths. At the same moment a small figure with half a dozen arms and legs whirled into the dining room from the area of the bathroom, capturing the attention of all three. It was Elijah, in flight. He scooted diagonally across the empty dining room, a pinwheel shooting sparks. Then his mother ran in too, her now unbraided satin hair streaming over her knapsack, a hunchbacked bird. "I'm going to get you!"

There was a swoop. The pinwheel was caught. But his captor was not the raven but the bat: Signe. She held him high, above her upturned face. He grinned down at her. Her cape hung in a column behind her. Elijah's mother skidded to a stop.

"My baby!" she demanded.

Rhea joined them.

"I a plane!" shouted Elijah, flapping his elbows. "Donna, I a plane!"

Rhea lifted her arms in imitation of her mother. Elijah's mother lifted her arms too. "My baby," she said, in a softer voice. Signe placed Elijah in the girdle formed by Rhea's hands. Rhea held the child aloft for a moment, then passed him to his mother. She too held him briefly like a chalice before settling him onto her shoulder and marching out.

Signe adjusted her cape. Then she turned to her daughter. They exchanged a long, silent stare—a gaze of peace and intimacy and intricately tangled pleasure. The space between them became briefly radiant. Donna, though blistered, watched. She wondered whether she would ever again pay honor to that meagre virtue getting-along-with-people. She knew that she would never again claim to understand anything about mothers and children.

They left. Donna walked into the kitchen. It would be a pleasure to stew tomatoes until they burst through their skins.

Home Schooling

Nauseated, dizzy, I lay on the back seat of our dusty car, my head resting against the garment bag that held my father's two tuxedos. Beyond my raised knees I saw a mortar sky. Above the front seat rose my Aunt Kate's pony-tailed head and shoulders, and my twin sister's head, or at least the top of her baseball cap. Willy kept fiddling with the radio and singing French songs we'd learned from our parents. "Yaagh," I said every so often.

"Feeling better, hon?" said Aunt Kate, not taking her eyes off the road. Yesterday, the day we'd left home, she'd quit her graduate program in Classics, chucked those Romans as if they were all losers. "Feeling the same?"

"Feeling worse."

"Let us know if you have to stop."

"I have to stop."

So at the next opportunity Aunt Kate pulled over. I sat on a hump of grass and thrust my head between my thighs. Aunt Kate stood nearby. Willy gazed at us from the car. "It might be better if you did throw up," she said, not unkindly. "Carsickness is your specialty."

"Vomiting is *not* my specialty," I reminded her, though I spoke into my skirt and probably couldn't be heard. I can still remember that ugly plaid, turquoise and peach. At the time—we were ten— I thought it gorgeous.

My carsickness had something to do with my inner ear, our pediatrician told us: I had an atypical vestibular canal. Willy's vestibular canal was less atypical, the doctor tactfully said, when pressed. More normal, better—but he didn't say those things. Who cared? I had a more atypical memory than Willy. That is, she remembered not a lot and I remembered almost everything.

Otherwise we were pretty similar in aptitudes and tastes, though we didn't look alike—I am dark and she is fair, I have a blunt short nose and she has a long thin one. In those days we both wore braids.

I didn't throw up, not once on the three-day journey to Boston. My father had thrown up at the beginning of his illness, when the headaches began. He was already in our new home while we were driving and I was not throwing up. Our new home was a rented flat in a three-decker section of the city. My parents had flown ahead with two suitcases and my father's violin.

When not in the hospital for treatments my father slept in the front bedroom with my mother. A congregation of mahogany furniture kept them company. On the highboy stood a stag line of Dad's medications. Mom's perfume bottles flared their hips at the pills.

Aunt Kate had the middle bedroom. Willy and I shared the

back room. Our window looked down on an oblong of brown earth rimmed with pink geraniums, an abcess of a yard. The view horizontally at our third-floor level was more encouraging—clapboard three-deckers like ours, their back bedrooms close enough to see into at night. These were children's rooms. We gave the children epithets: Nose Picker, Curls, Four-Eyes, Amaryllis. Amaryllis was a stalk of a girl with a beautiful drooping head. She was about thirteen. Beyond and between these nearer houses we could see bits of the other side of their street—more houses with front porches—and beyond that row still another set of back windows. "Like scenery," said Willy. I knew what she meant: the flat overlapping facades destroyed perspective, turned the daytime view into backdrop. At night, though, when the near windows were lit, the rooms behind them acquired depth, even intensity. Nose Picker practiced his perversion. Curls read magazines on her bed. Amaryllis smiled into the telephone.

There were black-bellied hibachis on some of the porches. It was the era of hibachis. It was the era of consciousness-raising. The previous year our third grade had been told that women could be anything they wanted to be. We were puzzled by this triumphant disclosure; nobody at home had hinted otherwise. It was the year of war protests and assassinations. Hubert Humphrey kissed his own face on a hotel TV screen. There were breakthroughs in cancer therapy.

Whenever my father went into the hospital for his treatments he had to share a room with some other patient—sometimes an old man, sometimes a young one. They too were recovering from surgery and receiving therapy. My father wore a turban, entirely white, though with no central jewel. He and Aunt Kate, siblings

105

but not twins, resembled each other more than Willy and I did—the same silky red hair, the same soft brown eyes. His eyes were dull, now, and his hair had vanished into his sultan's headgear.

Most mornings Willy and I found Kate and my mother at the kitchen table silently drinking coffee. During the fall some brown light made its way through the one spotted window; by winter the only light came from a table lamp: a dark little pot whose paper shade was veined like an old face. We owned no appliances—a fortunate deprivation, for the kitchen had no counters. We kept crockery and utensils in a freestanding cupboard, drawers below, shelves above. Our canned goods marshaled themselves on a ledge above an ecru enameled stove. The enamel had worn off the stove in some places; it looked like the hide of a sick beast. Kate and Mom said that the atypically patterned stove was a period piece, a survivor; they seemed to feel a pet-owner's affection for it.

A brand new refrigerator occupied most of the back hall. It was too big for the blackened space in our gypsy kitchen where a smaller refrigerator had once stood. In place of the vanished fridge my mother installed her teletype. She nailed corkboard onto the wall above the instrument. From the corkboard fluttered pages of computer code. The teletype was usually turned off in the morning, but when she was expecting a print-out she turned it on, and when we came into the kitchen we could hear its hum. During breakfast the thing would seem to square its shoulders against an onslaught. Then the message would begin to type out. Paper rose jerkily from the platen. Sometimes what scrolled into our kitchen was a copy of the program my mother was working on, with its three-letter instructions and fanciful addresses:

TAK FEEBLE

PUT FOIBLE

TRN ELSEWHERE

We knew that such a series represented the transfer first of information and then of control. We understood the octal number system and the binary number system and their eternal correspondence. Fractions and decimals, however, were still *terra incognita* to us; and Willy, invoking her not atypical memory, hadn't yet bothered to learn any method of long division.

At breakfast Mom and Kate wore flowered wrappers trimmed with lace. They lingered over their coffee as if they had all the daylight hours to kill. Early in the fall, when Dad was home more often, when he was still getting up for breakfast, he told them that they looked like demi-mondaines and that Willy and I looked like semi-demi-mondaines and that we were his harem and the teletype his eunuch.

When the New England winter settled in my mother bought oatmeal, and on those dark mornings it bubbled on the stove. We hated oatmeal. But it was the glue of normality, the stuff that was supposed to stick to kids' ribs through a morning of math and grammar. So we spooned some into bowls and joined our mother and our aunt at the round table. They had already divided the newspaper between them; now each divided her section with one of us. The teletype throbbed. Kate got up to pour more coffee. Her hips were as slim as a boy's. She sat down. The teletype spat. After a while Mom got up. She bent over the machine, hair falling forward, hand splayed on lace bosom.

It was not usual in those days for a programmer to have a

teletype installed in her home. But my mother was not a usual programmer. Her mind could sinuate into the circuitry of a machine. She understood its syntax and could make use of its simple doggy logic. "I have a modest gift," she earnestly told us. "I was just born with it, like freckles." Fifty years earlier—ten years earlier, even—a person with such a faculty would have had to divert it to accounting, or weaving, or puzzles. My mother had been born into the right generation for her talent. In that regard she was lucky.

She had landed a part-time job a week after our arrival. A month later she was offered the home teletype and told that she could work as many hours as she pleased, at twice the original rate of pay. She had to attend the weekly staff conference; that was the only requirement made of her. But she considered contact with her fellow workers important, and anyway she always did more than people asked. So she and we went into the office two days a week, often staying until midnight. On those days she'd visit my father in the morning, and then drive home to pick us up. I sat stiffly in the front seat and willed myself not to get carsick.

Computers were hulking giants then, with lights and switches and whirring magnetic tapes. Mom's machine growled in an air-conditioned warehouse, surrounded by a warren of offices with fiberboard walls and desks that were just planks on iron legs. Programmers hung snapshots and party invitations and straw hats above their desks. My mother's walls were bare; but in one corner of her office a pair of old school chairs with armrests sat at a thirty-degree angle to each other. She had picked them up in a secondhand shop near the hospital. Between the chairs stood an oversized tin bucket filled with books and games. Under it all was a small fake Oriental rug.

Home Schooling

Whenever I see the word *happiness* I think of that corner.

Few of Mom's co-workers were married, and none were parents. Some brought their dogs to work. One evening one of her fellow programmers took us to a wrestling match. We held our breaths each time a fighter was pinned, sighed when he was resurrected. Later in the year a young woman took us to the Flower Show. Clubs from the suburban towns had created real gardens in real earth in front of painted houses. We brought home a pot of daffodils and a paper poppy. "I will extract some paper opium from this," said our father in his weakened voice. "We will have such dreams... Dreams!" he suddenly shouted.

But field trips were rare. Mostly we spent Mom's workdays in our corner.

An elderly secretary labored for my mother's group. She kept conventional hours, and it was a while before we had any commerce with her. But one December afternoon at about five she stopped us on our way back from the sandwich machine. She was seated at her typewriter, and she didn't lift her fingertips from the keys when she spoke to us, though the tapping ceased. "Harriet and Wilma," she said by way of greeting.

All we had to do was say Hello Miss Masters and smile and skedaddle. But: "Harry and Willy," Willy corrected.

Miss Masters slid her hands onto her lap with an awful gravity. "Twins but not identical."

"Fraternal sisters," said Willy.

"What grade are you in?"

"Fourth," I said at the same time that Willy said "Fifth."

"My oh my" was the extent of Miss Master's reply, but her tone was inquisitorial.

"She's advanced," I said, my explanation ruinously coinciding with Willy's "She's retarded." Then we did skedaddle. When we'd turned a corner I grabbed Willy by her bony shoulder.

"Do you *want* to go to school?" I demanded.

"Jeez. No."

"Well, then."

My mother was sitting at her slab of a desk, writing code. Whenever she was bent over her work, her shoulder-length hair, abundant but limp, separated of its own accord and fell on either side of her neck. We settled down on our chairs with sandwiches and books, our presence unacknowledged. We understood that absorption, not indifference, made her ignore us, just as we understood that our father's sudden explosions were disease, not rage. My mother's pencil scratched. We read and chewed. She began to hum—a sign that she had solved a problem. She straightened and moved her chair outward, and it protested faintly, aagh. I looked up and began to sing the words to the tune my mother was humming. The song was "Good Morning" from the movie *Singin' in the Rain*—we'd seen it twice in the Revival House back home and once on somebody's television. Willy joined in, a third higher. We sang the words and Mom abandoned the melody and hummed continuo. The wrestling programmer, walking in with a flow diagram, stopped to listen to this makeshift serenade.

When we didn't go to work with Mom we went to work with Kate. After my mother left for the hospital, after we had finished the housecleaning (Kate wore a blue bandanna over her hair) and had made a trip to the library and the Civil War Monument and had perhaps listened to the organist practice in the little brick church

110

or visited chilly Walden Pond, traveling by bus, or inspected the daily catch up in Gloucester, traveling by train, or curled up at home, listening to our aunt read her own translation of Ovid . . . after that, we set off for the Busy Bee Diner. Aunt Kate did a half-shift at the Busy Bee, from four until eight.

On our walk to the diner we saw the children of the neighborhood engaged in their various childish activities: practicing hoop shots, or minding toddlers, or, at the variety store, fastening powerful gazes onto the candy counter so that Baby Ruths would leap into their pockets. Often we recognized the young people we'd spied on from our window—Nose Picker, his hands safe in his pockets; Curls, pretty; Amaryllis, gorgeous. Other kids, too. They wore hand-me-down clothes and they looked strictly brought up. They were all white, and most were fair. Not Amaryllis, though. Dark brows shaded dark eyes: a Mediterranean siren in this Hibernian tract.

We looked at the familiar strangers, and they looked back at us. Did they wonder about us? Parochial School students probably thought we went to Public School. The Public Schoolers knew we had never been seen in their cinder-block building; did they notice that we didn't wear the pleated skirts and white blouses of Catholic scholars? How did they explain us to each other? We speculated about their speculations.

"Because of our delicate health we are tutored at home," suggested Willy.

"By our aged relative," I added.

Aunt Kate grinned.

The Busy Bee was owned and manned by the Halasz family. The Halasz rice pudding was made with ricotta; the Halasz chocolate pie contained nuggets of chocolate cake. When my father was out of stir, as Kate called it, we would bring home one of these desserts, and also a carton of barley beef stew. Though the food was very good, he didn't finish it.

We longed to practice short-order cooking behind the counter with Milo Halasz, and to try waitressing with Kate. But laws against Child Labor were more severe than laws against Truancy. Mr. Halasz allowed us to work only in the kitchen, a high square room that the public couldn't see. Mr. Halasz, who wore a beret as a chef's hat, taught us to scrub up like surgeons. He taught us to pound herbs and then powder them between our palms, and to roll leaves of cabbage around chopped meat sweetened with rosemary, and to beat egg whites until they were as stiff as bandage gauze.

Some mornings Kate visited my father while my mother stayed home with us and the eunuch. We didn't resent not being left on our own. We knew that our competence was not in question, just as we knew that it was not hatred of men that caused Aunt Kate to snub the blameless advances made by some of the Busy Bee's patrons, and to keep Milo at arm's length too; and that it was not Willy's skinniness that prompted Mom to lay her cheek against my sister's some wintry mornings in the living room, and it was not my tendency to vertigo that made her embrace me suddenly in the kitchen. And although Willy and I liked to check on what the neighbors were up to, it was not to watch Amaryllis brushing her hair that we perfected our spying techniques. It was to watch our two demi-mondaines. We saw the glances they exchanged in the beginning of that year; and then we sensed glances without seeing them; and eventually we sensed glances they didn't even need to exchange.

Often I got up at night—to use the bathroom, if anybody

asked—but really to draw closer to the dark heat in the living room. Sometimes Aunt Kate played Chopin or Schubert on the upright. Usually she lay on the couch, her knees bent, reading. Mom sat at the desk, coding. Music came from the hi-fi; Rosamunde, Egmont, Siegfied. The two women talked a little. One time, without preamble, my mother got up from the desk and crossed the room and dropped to the floor and laid her head on Aunt Kate's abdomen. She began soundlessly to cry. Aunt Kate placed the book she'd been reading, still open, across her own forehead, like a sombrero. She held it there with her left hand as if against a gale. With her right hand she fondled my mother's foolish hair.

In March my father was transferred to a Rehabilitation Center. One Saturday afternoon my mother took us to see him there. We drove across the city. The place was near grim buildings of mostly undefinable uses, though one of them, we knew, was a popular roller-skating rink.

Dad was not connected to an IV. "A free pigeon," he said, flapping his elbows. His gait was unsteady but he could walk without a cane and without leaning too much on my mother—his arm around her shoulders was mostly an embrace. The four of us tramped up and down the corridors, as if not daring to stop. I think he guessed what was coming—the tumor's steady growth, the blindness in the right eye, the new operation, the new operation's failure... Along the polished linoleum the sick man marched, whispering into his wife's ear. Her hair separated, revealing her meek nape. We trailed behind.

At four-thirty my parents finally sat down on my father's bed.

They were going to share supper in the cafeteria, they said. It was always nutritionally appropriate. "Bilious," Dad confided. "Maybe you two would like to go out for pizza."

If we stayed we could watch her eat, watch him pretend to eat, eat ourselves, see! good children, swallowing the meat loaf, the stewed fruit. "But…" Willy began.

"Have fun," said my mother.

We trudged down the corridor. In each room lay two sad patients.

The pizza parlor had tiled walls and a feral odor. There were no booths, only tables. It was too early for the supper crowd. Except for a few solitaries in windbreakers we were the only customers. We ordered our pizza and sat down to wait for it.

Four girls burst in. They must have traveled by trolley and underground to get here. Roller skates hung from their shoulders. Amaryllis's were packed in a denim case.

"Hello," they said.

"Hello," we said.

They swept to the counter to order their pizzas. We studied their various backs—erect, round-shouldered, slim, bisected by a braid—and their various stances—jumpy, slouching, queenly, hands in back pockets—and their noses as they turned their profiles this way and that, and their languor or purpose as they visited the jukebox or the ladies' room, and their ease as they more or less assembled at their table, one always getting up for something, where are the napkins anyway, talking, laughing, heads together, heads apart, elbows gliding on the table. The girl with glasses—I was pretty sure her name was Jennifer, so many girls were Jennifers—sat in a way that was familiar to me, her right knee bent outwards so that her right foot could rest

114

on the chair, her left thigh keeping the foot in place like a brick on a pudding; this position caused a deep satisfying cramp; I knew that pain. "Wilma," called the pizza man. Willy got up to get our pizza. The girls didn't watch her. Willy brought the pizza to our table, and we divided it, along with our salad. "Nicole," the pizza man said. The girl I'd thought of as Jennifer uncoiled and went to fetch the pizzas with Amaryllis. Nicole and Amaryllis set the big round pies carefully on the table. Then came an unseemly scramble. They laughed, and grabbed, and accused each other of greed, and somebody spilled a Coke. "Pig!" they cried. "Look who's talking." "Jen, you thief," laughed the bespectacled Nicole as Amaryllis overturned one wedge of pizza onto another, making a sandwich of it, doubling her first portion. "Jen, you cow!"

So Amaryllis was just another Jennifer. She raised her face. She was wearing a tomato sauce mustache, beautifying. She looked directly at me. Then she looked directly at Willy. Four-Eyes— Nicole—raised her head too and followed Amaryllis's gaze—Jen's gaze. Then the third girl. Then the fourth.

We were all over them in a minute. We swarmed, if two boyish eleven-year-olds can be said to swarm over a quartet of nubile adolescents. Eleven-year-olds? Yes; we had celebrated our birthday the month before. We were officially teenagers, my father had said from his bed in the front room (he was out of stir, that weekend), handing us each a leather diary, one brown, one blue. Any number between eleven and nineteen, inclusive, belonged in the teens mathematically, my mother explained; we might call ourselves one-ten or one-teen if we liked. Many languages used that locution, said Aunt Kate.

We were one-ten; this interesting fact we told our new friends.

115

We talked about pizza toppings. We discussed television programs we'd never seen. Boys in the neighborhood too. "You know Kevin?" Nicole asked.

"I know who he is," I lied. "Wicked." We knew that wicked meant splendid.

Did we like the Stones? Harrison Ford? Had we ever seen the gas meter man?

No one asked us what grade we were in.

Did we skate?

Skating was our passion, Willy said. We had practically been born on little steel wheels. Next to watching television and plucking our eyebrows...

"We come to the rink on a lot of Saturdays," said Amaryllis, who would never be Jen to me. She stood up, and her associates stood with her. "Maybe we'll see you here some time. Here."

Hear, hear: here. Any further commerce between us would be off-neighborhood. We got it: we were known in their homes, and not thought well of. Maybe their families had glimpsed the whorish dressing gowns of our mother and aunt. Perhaps they were prejudiced against men in turbans.

The schoolgirls whirled out. Willy and I shuffled back to the hospital. My mother was waiting for us in the dim lobby. We three walked wordlessly to the car.

In the late spring he came home for the last time. He couldn't eat, unless you count tea. "I'd like to play a little," he said to Kate.

Whenever the quartet or the symphony performed he sat up on the stage, remote. Once, though, he had fiddled almost in our midst, at the wedding of my mother's youngest brother; standing,

116

he played "The Anniversary Waltz" by request, borrowing an instrument from the hired trio. He was wearing his tuxedo on that occasion, and his red hair above the black-and-white garment gave him a hectic gaiety. My mother told us that "The Anniversary Waltz" was an old Russian tune, stolen and given words in order to fill a need in a movie musical.

In our rented living room my father did not play "The Anniversary Waltz." He played a few sweet things—some Mendelssohn and some Gluck—and Aunt Kate did well with the accompaniment; very well, really, since she was silently sobbing. Then he played "Isn't It Romantic?" and Kate recovered and pushed through with a nice solo bit, Oscar Peterson-ish. We knew the tune and the lyrics, and we could have hummed along or even sung along. But we sat mute on the sofa, flanking our mother. Outside the street lamps illuminated the cardboard facades of the other houses. The sky was purple. My father wore a striped hospital robe over custard pajamas. His eyes closed when he reached the final note. Silence. From the kitchen the teletype began to clatter.

"No dependent clauses," said the principal back home, in August. "No Middle Ages." She was muttering, but in a kindly fashion. She was trying to decide whether to enroll us in the fourth grade or simply to declare it skipped. "Tell me what you did learn."

Willy sat looking out of the window at the playground. I sat looking at Willy. "What did you learn?" the principal gently repeated.

We kept mum. So we had to repeat fourth grade, or endure it for the first time, who cared, same difference. Willy did master long division. I never figured out how to forget.

Shenanigans

"Hildy's mother, she must be wondrously preponderate," said Devlin's mother.

"Preponderate? That's no word."

"'Tis. 'Twas a verb, but it raised itself to an adjective. Scrabble is a fine university. I'm dying to meet her, Hildy Tartakoff's mother. Lillian, she's called, or so I believe." And Devlin's mother twinkled at her son like an entire constellation. These damned Celtic mannerisms, he thought; they seemed to be an affliction of her old age. Other people's parents descended sorrowfully into Alzheimer's; his was turning into a leprechaun.

Meanwhile, Hildy Tartakoff's mother—she *was* called Lillian—was saying in an offhand manner that she'd like to meet Devlin's mother. "That is, if your affair is going to continue. And I must admit," she chummily elaborated, "I'd be disappointed if it didn't do that."

"If what didn't do which?" Hildy asked.

119

"If the romance didn't go on. So shouldn't we meet, she and I?" Lillian reasonably wound up.

No one could argue with her mother's logic, Hildy knew, since there was never any logic to argue with. There was merely determination masquerading as syllogism. Lillian had held sway over many organizations using this rhetorical principle.

"Shall I call her Laura?" Lillian asked.

"If you like," sighed the defeated Hildy. "Her name is Maura, though."

So Devlin Fitzgerald—whose affair with Hildy Tartakoff *was* continuing, at least for now—arranged a luncheon for four in his hotel on the border of Godolphin and Boston—a small hotel in the European style, the advertisements ran, though such embodiments of subtle hospitality were getting rare even in Europe. Christmas was coming. Abundant greenery, though not a touch of tinsel, decorated the carpeted reception hall. A fire blazed in a marble hearth. Off to one side was the private dining room. There, Dev and Maura awaited their guests.

As a young man busily creating his now renowned hotel, Devlin had married a good-tempered woman who remained good-tempered through decades of neglect. But after their two daughters were grown she left him for a retired army officer who liked to putter around his *own* house. Granny Maura stayed friendly with the woman she still called her daughter-in-law. "Ex is not in me alphabet," she was fond of saying, Irishing her conversation in that irritating way.

For this special meeting she was dressed in a gray wool dress with a white lace collar, and Dev could have murdered her. He knew, because he had paid for them, that she owned a couple of Armani knock-offs; why couldn't she have worn one of those? Lillian would arrive looking authoritative as usual, handsome, even military. He admired Lillian, from whom Hildy inherited her height, her rich hair (graying on the daughter's head, resolutely dark on the mother's), her energy, her cleverness. Hildy's green eyes came from her deceased father; her extra weight—twenty pounds, Devlin estimated—was her own doing. She was a high-school guidance counselor. Twenty year ago she had endured a brief, childless marriage. She and her husband had bickered all the time, she told Dev, eyes amused, or maybe reflective, or perhaps even yearning.

Lillian in old age (Late Middle was the term she preferred) still walked several miles every morning, a slender figure in corduroys and a sweater. After this workout she got dressed in some fashionable outfit, its skirt at whatever length Milan decreed—so it was a shock to Devlin when she entered the room in an old lady's dress that was almost a dead ringer for Maura's, brown rather than gray, a necklace of amber beads rather than a collar, but still...you'd think the two birds had conferred ahead of time, were up to something.

"My dear Mrs. Fitzgerald," said Lillian without waiting to be introduced.

"Mrs. Tartakoff, me dear dear," said Maura.

They were each other's destiny, hinted the tall old Jewess. The tiny flower of Erin concurred. Over the soup they decided to attend the Yo Yo Ma concert together next week; they'd use Lillian's tickets and scalp Maura's. They'd go to the Foxwoods Casino in January, they settled over the chicken. Lillian liked blackjack—she was an expert

121

card counter. Maura preferred roulette. This difference in taste would not come between them, they predicted. And—they discovered while spooning up dessert—their apartments were less than two miles apart. "Is that not a coincidence?" demanded Lillian.

"Lillian," said Devlin, producing what he hoped was a chuckle; "Godolphin measures two miles by three; most people live . . ."

"Yes, dearie," interrupted Maura, "but *my* being in Godolphin in the first place—that's the astounding complementarity." A decade earlier Maura had finally agreed to move out of the shabby South Boston house she'd raised her family in. But a retirement community?—"Over my corpse." She allowed Devlin to pay the rent on a first-floor flat near the Godolphin fire station. "Visiting nurses; be off with you. I can manage injections on me own." And she could, and did, testing her glucose with one of those disposable finger sticks she carried in her purse, then uncapping the one-dose insulin syringe, sticking the thing into a convenient bit of flesh. Her son had seen her perform this routine several times at a restaurant, God help him, God help her: she glanced at the blood-sugar reading while other people were inspecting their menus; yes, too high; she unbuttoned the lowest button on her silk blouse and stabbed herself in the stomach and buttoned up again. No one ever noticed the exercise except his horrified self. Once she injected herself *through* the garment, then winked at him.

"You live only two miles from my house—just think of it," said Maura to Lillian.

"I'll walk over sometime," said Lillian to Maura.

"Tomorrow, then," said Maura.

"Tomorrow," said Lillian.

Dev poured more wine.

122

Shenanigans

"I don't drink at lunch," said Hildy. "Well, never more than one," she corrected, draining her second glass.

"I'm the one who deserves to be diabetic," said Lillian to Maura about a month later. "I'm Jewish and I'm eighty-five."

"Eighty-five, exactly my age," said Maura, who was eighty-six.

Lillian suffered only from high cholesterol and occasional cavities. The admiring Maura had taken up walking under Lillian's influence. They met Wednesdays and Fridays out at the Reservoir and circled it three times, Lillian looking like a long wading bird, Maura resembling a sandpiper.

Under Maura's influence Lillian had recovered an interest in whisky. She now repudiated white wine. "The stuff's just grape juice, when you come right down to it," she announced.

"What do those two talk about, do you think?" Devlin asked Hildy. It was a Thursday night; they were meeting for a hamburg in a tavern before Devlin went back to the hotel to inspect some new fabrics and Hildy went back to her desk to write references for last-minute college applications.

"Our mothers? They talk about us, Dev. My mother talks about how elegant and cultivated you are." She watched him lightly preen. Well, shouldn't he be proud, she inquired of her critical side: he reads novels in French; he attends early music concerts; he flavors this mixture with regular attendance at boxing matches...

"And distinguished," added Hildy, baiting him without his noticing. "What about *your* mother," she asked. "What does she say about me?"

He considered the question, bending on her the fine dark gaze that made hotel visitors feel singled out for attention, that made the hotel staff want to die in his service, that made his daughters forgive him his absences because his presences were so satisfying. "She thinks you have the world's most interesting eyes. She wants an ornament made exactly of that pale jade."

Hildy grew warm.

"And she finds your insights keen," Dev went on.

Hildy grew warmer still, though it might just be her uncomfortable time of life—hot flashes, and extra weight, and the Lord knew what was happening to *her* cholesterol. "Maura probably thinks I'm fat," Hildly said in a light tone.

"No, no," Devlin assured her.

"Yes, yes."

"Maybe, maybe. A few pounds." How stunning she'd look in a velvet dress the color of eucalyptus he'd seen in a window; but the garment needed lissomeness...

"Damn, damn," said Hildy.

"*I* think you're perfect," said Devlin in the tone of a forced convert. Hildy, who had planned to leave her French fries untouched on her plate, now began to pick them up one by one, in silence. She was not usually silent. She could do the talking for both of them, he reflected; he was basically unsociable, though because he kept a hotel he had to pretend otherwise. He imagined that they would grow old together with a minimum of regrets.

He might have told her this—it would have saved the evening. But he had blarneyed enough, and she was still eating those fries, one after the other.

Lillian's big apartment was decorated in colors that Maura thought of as Pallor, Jaundice, and Congestive Failure. (Maura had worked as a

Nurse's Aid while the kids were growing up. ("My mother is retired from the health profession," she'd heard that scamp of a boy say; such airs.) At Lillian's place the two women often played Scrabble and talked about movies. At Maura's—bright yellow walls, a tiled fireplace—they played gin rummy and recalled their childhoods.

"People sussurate about the emerald hills," said Maura. "But what I remember most favorably is the stone houses and the Liffey, slow as vaseline."

"In my time New York was swarming with Socialists," said Lillian. "My parents were Reds, if you want to know the utter truth."

"Utter truth, there's no such thing. I'll knock with three."

Meanwhile Dev and Hildy talked about where they might live—her little house, so comfortable, his flat at the top of the hotel, so handy. They talked about which gubernatorial candidate was most deserving of their vote, the district attorney full of righteous indignation ("he hounds people," said Hildy) or the ex-cop, a charming rogue ("up to his nose in debt," said Dev). The Red Sox lineup—each would have rearranged it, but differently. Their discussions sometimes subsided into lovemaking and more often flared into fights—that is, Hildy fought, Devlin grew silent.

"Conflict is the stuff of life," Maura reminded her son. His handsome face grew stony. "You always sidestepped trouble," she sighed.

"You don't have to defend every damned one of your principles," said Lillian to Hildy. "Swallow some of them; they'll go down like Jello." Then she stopped talking. It was too late to teach her daughter the value of hypocrisy.

And after a while Hildy and Dev, the one delighting in battle and the other craving peace—acknowledged their differences and broke up.

Maura, hearing this awful news, hastened on foot to Hildy's house, ablaze in the spring evening. "You have broken my heart," she shouted when Hildy opened the door.

"Will you have some tea? Devlin and I ..."

"Whisky."

"...are too unalike in psychological stance, in cognitive style ..."

"Ice cubes are an abomination."

"...to remain together," continued Hildy, trying to remove the offending ice with a spoon and then using her fingers. She handed the glass to Maura. "Devlin is interested in how things seem, I am interested in how things are. He caters to guests' physical needs, I to students' emotional wants ..."

"Yobba, yobba, stop blathering."

Hildy, who had been about to drink a cup of heavily sugared tea, abruptly dosed it with whisky. They were both standing in the kitchen, and Maura was still wearing her coat.

"You're a pair of stubborn cockerels," said Maura. "Don't you know that differences bring us together? Or do you want to marry somebody just like you? Your own self, if you can manage it. A clone with a dong."

Hildy sighed. Oh, she would miss this fearsome old lady. "That's not what I want, really ..."

"It's Devlin who should marry your own self. You're soft and merry, when you leave off psychologizing and that. Make it up, girl."

Hildy stuck her finger in the adulterated and now cooling tea and rapidly stirred. "We'll all stay friends," she said in a weak voice.

Meanwhile, Lillian was rushing by taxi to the hotel. "Mr. Fitzgerald is at the Chamber of Commerce meeting," said the night manager. She took another taxi to Town Hall. She slipped into the back row of the meeting room. They were discussing the soup kitchen in the basement of the Unitarian Church. Some Yankee stood up to defend the facility. Devlin rose next, defending it also, and with energy. He could argue when he wanted to, couldn't he. His shoulder in that well-cut jacket, his cleft chin, that little flag of eyelashes... Lillian sat straighter, sucked in her stomach.

He turned as he was about to sit down, and saw her. He glided out of his row and into hers. He kissed her on the cheek. She turned to him, suddenly breathless, and clutched his upper arms. "Dev!"

"Is the Chamber to have the benefit of your fabled energy?" he asked.

"Forget the smooth talk. Call off the calling off."

"We'd make each other miserable, she so intense, me so... cautious."

"Paralyzed," she said, and watched him stiffen. "Oh, Dev, you're the son-in-law I always wanted," in a gentler voice.

He sighed. "Mr. Fitzgerald?" called the chairman.

"I've got to make a presentation," said Dev gratefully. He kissed Lillian again and slid away. She sat there for a few minutes, still feeling the touch of his lips.

Then she got up and called a third cab. She arrived at Maura's just as that lady was stumbling up her front stairs.

"What can we do?" Lillian cried.

"We'll think of something," said Maura. "Could you help me with this key, now."

127

The next morning Maura's daughter's daughter bore a daughter out in Cincinnati; and not until four days later, on the plane headed back home, did she have time to put her mind to the problem. "Whatever we do they'll call it intrusion," Lillian had groaned. "Intrusion's a mortal sin."

But—Maura thought while unpacking—didn't Hildy and Devlin require some gentle intrusion, if that phrase wasn't what people called a pachyderm, no, oxyderm, well, something like that.

She heard fire engines. They were always shrieking; usually it was somebody's heart attack. What a darling great-granddaughter, that child in Ohio, Maura was her name, the fourth Maura in a row. Let the girl have the happiness I've had, thought Maura; and, happy, got into bed.

Ten hours later, as she was uncapping her insulin, the telephone rang. "I'm in Godolphin Rehab," said Lillian's voice on the telephone. She sounded as strong as usual.

"Good will mission?" asked Maura.

"Chest pains," Lillian thundered. "But the big Boston Teaching Hospital couldn't find anything wrong so they transferred me here."

"Dearie!"

"Oh, unlikely to be significant. But my young doctor worries when ancients like us get sick. And here he comes. I'd better get my feet back under the . . . blankets. Oh, hello," she said to somebody.

"I can hardly hear you all of a sudden," shouted Maura. "Is something wrong with the telephone?"

"Not with the telephone," said Lillian feebly. "I'll talk . . . later."

The person Lillian called her young doctor was one year short of retirement. He was confounded by his patient: sallow, tight-lipped, reporting pain. His examination revealed nothing. His equipment failed to register a complaint.

"My feet are so cold," wailed Lillian.

He reached under the covers and felt their iciness, patted them in his kindly way, and found the drawer where nurses kept heavy socks. "And the chest pains?" he said, slipping the footwarmers onto her feet.

"Come, go, come, go."

"I'll be back in an hour," he said; and an hour later he was back. "You look a little better."

"Much worse," she assured him.

"Well, we'll keep monitoring you."

"Send me home, I'll die there."

He scowled. "I won't send..."

There was a disturbance outside the room; a kind of screeching on the linoleum. Then: "Where is she? Lillian, where are you!" and a white-faced glistening little woman tottered through the doorway and collapsed onto the patient.

It took a while to get her off—indeed, the patient seemed to be convulsively holding on to the assailant. When the staff did manage to peel the small woman from the large one they discovered that the newcomer was in diabetic distress.

"Let me expire next to Lillian," she gasped.

"You're not expiring," said an elderly nurse with orange hair. "And I know that Mrs. Tartakoff would prefer a single room..."

"No, no!" shouted Lillian. "No, no," she repeated in a sickly voice. "Mrs. Fitzgerald must stay."

"...and the TV for the second bed isn't working," said the nurse.

"Oh, oh, and me favorite program!" cried Maura.

"We'll get it fixed." Attention turned to the broken TV. Maura lay down while her glucose was regulated; but she insisted on getting up to unpack the nightcase she had presciently brought. An aide spotted a brown bottle underneath the pink nightclothes. She thought of reporting this infraction; but she was going off her shift, and her boyfriend was waiting . . .

By midafternoon the second television, at last repaired, flashed some anchor's frosted grin. "Marvelous," said Maura, and clicked it off.

Each patient had a book. Each lay quiet, reading.

Firm footsteps sounded in the hall.

"Wssht," said Maura.

Lillian reached into her drawer and found her sleep mask and slipped it over her eyes. For good measure she turned her head into the pillow, though she left an ear exposed.

But Devlin didn't even glance at the first patient. He walked swiftly toward the second one, the one near the window, the one whose quilted bedjacket he had supplied himself a few Christmases ago.

"Mother," said the thrilling voice.

"Darlin'," said Maura. "Twitch that curtain."

The glide of the curtain reached Lillian's ear. Cautiously she raised her mask. Below the curtain now concealing the other bed she saw the backs of dark brown trousers and dark brown shoes. The trouser cuffs lifted ever so slightly. He must be bending over her. They must be embracing.

Then the feet walked to the end of the bed. Then they returned, four metal legs following them like a dog. Man and chair halted;

130

then he apparently sat down. One trouser leg disappeared—that familiar, easy placement of ankle onto knee.

The voices grew low.

Ten minutes later Lillian heard new footsteps. Working woman's sneakers, she'd know them anywhere. She reached toward her bedside radio. Rachmaninoff. She lowered her lids. Her daughter's perfume filled her nostrils. She raised her lids. "Darling," she whispered to those green eyes.

"Darling," Hildy whispered back. "Why didn't someone call me yesterday? How are you feeling? What happened?"

"What happened, happened," said Lillian, still softly. "You're not wearing any lipstick; put some on." Her voice did not rise in volume; but it acquired the timbre that had once commanded the entire Women's Auxiliary. Hildy frowned. "For me," Lillian added, plaintive now, hand moving fast to her chest.

Lillian herself looked green without her usual rouge, thought Hildy. She rummaged in her briefcase and brought out a lipstick and half a mirror; who knew, this might be a deathbed request. "There's not enough light," she muttered.

And so it was with mirror raised in the left hand to catch the light from the hall, head thrown back, hair swinging, right arm curved to apply the make-up, though it might have been embracing a lover—it was a woman in this elemental pose that Devlin, turning in his chair, saw, just after Lillian, leaning recklessly out of bed, yanked the curtain open.

"Hildy?"

She paused in her beautifying. "Dev?"

They exchanged a long, serious, and ultimately annoyed look.

Each turned to the other's parent.

"What are you up to, Maura?" said Hildy.

"Lillian, this is my busy season," said Dev.

"Be quiet," said Maura. "Hildy, I'm a selfish old thing. I wanted you for me final illness. I wanted to lay me head on your deep breast. Ah, such machinations." She closed her eyes.

Hildy looked down at her own lap.

Devlin gazed directly at Lillian.

She gazed back.

Oh, if only she dared speak her unseemly thoughts. The deep corners of your mouth, she'd say; the cut of your Italian suit; those mahogany eyes. I wanted just an occasional kiss on my cheek and a sometime glimpse of the shoulders, of the eyes. We are satisfied with so little, we weary ones; imagination and memory does the rest. But without that little we're as good as gone.

Lillian merely ran her tongue over her silent lips.

After a while Devlin said, "Are you both all right? Really?"

"Really," sighed Maura, her eyes still closed.

"Really," said Lillian, though she knew herself to be an old lady at last.

So the former lovers left the room, Devlin motioning Hildy to precede him. They stayed together until the parking lot. There they parted.

Maura wriggled out of bed. She took a deck of cards from her suitcase. "Thank God for Insurance. I've stayed in worse places."

They played gin rummy until midnight.

Madame Guralnik

F leurs de trash," said Helene to her great-nephew. "Sprouting all over the place."

"What are you talking about, Tante Helene; and can I pour you some coffee?"

Sweet kid. "Come see for yourself," she said.

The kid—he was thirty—got up from the breakfast table and sauntered to the window. Had he lifted his pale eyes and swiveled them slightly, he could have seen the YMCA tower and beyond it the turrets of the Old City. But like his great-aunt he looked down at the street.

On the curb in front of the building stood a couple of garbage cans. Across them a stuffed trash bag rested like a corpse; on top of that lay a cardboard box. On the flap of the box someone had arranged three banana peels. They looked like flowers with golden petals. *"Fleurs de* trash," echoed Toby.

Helene's great-niece, Toby's first cousin, who had soundlessly

133

entered the room a few minutes earlier, joined them at the window. "Artistic," she said.

The sanitation workers' strike was in its third smelly day. Garbage rose in front of each apartment house, garbage crowned with gifts from passers-by: tilted soda bottles, paper bags humping like rodents, an old straw hat. Most citizens expected that the Mayor would settle the affair soon, even though yesterday he and the Chief Sanitation Engineer had called each other names in front of news cameras.

Helene glared at the banana peels. Artistic? Ah, all sorts of oddities passed for art these days. Last month the Israel Museum had exhibited sculptures formed out of shredded plastic bags and crushed tinfoil and bits of rope. From this debris the artiste had constructed life-sized simulacra of Moshe Dayan and Golda and of representative figures too—a rich man in an astrakhan; a rabbi; a bent schnorrer who might have walked out of Helene's Belgian childhood: give the man a coin, Lenya. The sculptress herself wore a dark green satin dress as shiny as a trash bag, designed by a clever Parisian. The *haute monde* of Jerusalem, hennaed to its roots, glided from form to form ...

"The street looks like Bombay," Angelica remarked.

"Harlem," said Toby.

"East Jerusalem," said Helene.

They drifted to the breakfast table—mustached Toby, who brokered businesses in New York; languid Angelica, married to a moneyed Indian; and Helene, at seventy-three the only remnant of her generation.

She was head of the clan. The large apartment was the family seat. Every Tuesday a Moroccan woman pretended to clean it. The other days Helene furtively scraped and scrubbed. On her knees!—this pampered youngest child of the proud Antwerp family who fled to Palestine, all six, just in time, with diamonds hastily sewn into their hems. Little Helene, dancing down the gangplank, smuggled one special gem in her rabbit muff.

Her brothers fought in the '48 war. Afterwards, for each in turn, Papa transformed a few diamonds into cash; then they went off to seek their fortunes in America, in France. Oh, how rich they got. Helene stayed with Mama and Papa in this very apartment in this very building, graced today with a mound of trash. Her parents, lean and erect as royalty, continued to mourn the cousins who had been left behind on the Keizerstraat, the friends who had flown into the arms of the Germans. What could you do.

Her parents were dead, her brothers also. And now the children of those dead brothers traveled to see her: men and women already in their fifties. They came: and *their* children came too—Toby and Angelica and a dozen others. Some of Papa's grandchildren even brought their own kiddies, not noticing the childless Helene's meagre enthusiasm. She was the Tante, wasn't she?—and so the fourth generation arrived to pay homage to her and to kiss the soil of Eretz Yisrael, avoiding of course the explosives, and the thugs, and the trash.

Toby poured coffee. Angelica arranged a plate of pastries. Toby put a little velvet pillow behind Helene's back. Angelica handed her yesterday's *Le Monde*. "You look ravishing," the girl whispered in her ear. (The girl was thirty-one.)

"You like my dressing gown?" Its deep V revealed a cameo on a chain: a woman in profile. "The cameo? Pretty junk; I've had it forever. I would lounge *en deshabille* all day if we weren't going to the airport. The cab comes at two."

They were leaving Jerusalem for Istanbul; they were off on a cut-rate gambling weekend sponsored by the Turkish government—plane tickets and hotel rooms for next-to-nothing. The wily Turks figured they'd get their money back at the tables. Toby was looking forward to a cautious flutter. Angelica had never been to Istanbul. And Helene? "Roulette I can take or leave," she said when the weekend was proposed. Who proposed it? Nobody remembered. "But it's another chance to visit Madame Guralnik. Maybe the last chance."

The entire family knew of this lady: Mama's young confidante, who set out for Haifa, and ended up in Salonika, and after that Istanbul, which we still called Constantinople. "Regina Guralnik, the prettiest woman in Antwerp," Helene often said. In fact, she hardly remembered Regina Guralnik in her heyday, but a photograph assisted memory or maybe replaced it. Madame Guralnik gazed tenderly into the wings of some photographer's studio; against the drapery her girlish profile glowed. A small, tiered hat leaned forward over the blonde bangs as if about to pitch itself onto the enchanting nose.

"Madame Guralnik must be a great age now," said Angelica.

"Very old, very wise, all that stuff."

"What does Madame live on these days?" asked Toby. It was two o'clock. They were waiting on the sidewalk for the cab.

"She deals in spices."

"Commodities?"

"A little shop, *cheri*. In Antwerp her father sold tinned fish," and then the white van pulled up. They had to circle the trash to get to its door. Helene motioned to the young people to go first. She followed, clutching an alligator overnight case. She wore a long black silk coat; scarf, shoes, and gloves were black too. Black mascara. How brilliant this early spring, she thought, just before ducking her champagne head to enter the cab—the almond trees had recently puffed into blossom.

The trash, *their* trash, had acquired a basket of rotting vegetables.

Helene slammed the door; the cab sped down the street. In the overheated interior dozing passengers were awakened by Angelica's good looks. A father and son stared. Two middle-aged women sniffed; for a moment Helene saw Papa's older sisters, imperiously waving away claimants for their valuable hands. An old man in a skullcap withdrew into his coat; and where did he think he was going on Erev Shabbat—was plane travel all of a sudden permitted? He was hopping to Cyprus, maybe; he'd get there before sundown and pray for the safe conclusion of his business whatever it was; probably computers; these days the Orthodox were deserting diamonds for electronics. One chip, another chip, they all made money.

At the airport Toby paid the fares. "A good deal, this shared cab," he commended with the thrift of a millionaire. Her father, his great-grandfather, would have agreed. "The greatest bargain, Helene, is the thing you *don't* buy," Papa liked to say. He was too large for bargains, too large for haggling. He had a weakness for fancies, though—pink marquises, yellow brilliants. "I bought them. I hid them. They escaped with us. Powerful stones, Lenya."

"Yes," she'd said, obedient as always to the suffering in his voice. Her own voice echoed in the stone vault of the Jerusalem bank. She was then eighteen.

"The green one, it's lucky. It rode in your muff."

"On the ship... I thought we were taking a vacation," she remembered wonderingly.

"Keep it always."

"In this bank? As if it didn't exist?"

He shrugged. "Who exists?"

Airport security lasted an age; what else was new. Angelica, despite her French passport, was asked about India, and about Pakistan, too. Perhaps she had a bomb in that sac, documents in the lining of her cape...

Helene next. No fuss. "Good luck," offered the security agent, her eyes already caressing Toby.

A crowd of Rumanians had commandeered the waiting area. The men's hair hung in greasy spirals, the women's wrists and fingers sparkled with colored glass. "God has a soft spot for the vulgar," Papa had told her. The whole crowd was already drunk, and on the plane they fought over the space in the overhead rack: you'd think it was the Golan. Helene stowed her own case under the chair in front. Seated, she slowly unwound her scarf; then, as if in an afterthought, she pulled off her gloves, finger by finger, and dreamily placed them in the bottom of her handbag. She fingered the cameo under her blouse. She buckled up and closed her eyes. She heard the roar of take-off; the calm tones of the pilot; the tinkle of the bar cart; the Rumanians, arguing... She opened her eyes.

And met Toby's blue ones. "Monsieur Guralnik?" he inquired.

She blinked and swallowed. "Died in Salonika."

"She is alone, then."

"Not any more. For the second husband she took a Turk."

"Adaptable," said Toby.

"We Belgians," sighed Helene.

They gambled that night, stretching modest investments into an hour of pleasure. Toby was the last to lose. Angelica and Helene stood behind him as the croupier raked away his final chip. Then the three left, smiling—handsome Toby, gorgeous Angelica, black-gloved Helene, each poorer now by a few dollars, rupees, shekels. The Turks would not recoup their investment in *this* threesome. But two Rumanians were sitting at the bar with their heads in their hands.

"Anything is better than the priests," said their guide. She was a university student, poorly dressed. "Yes, I can tolerate the military; we suffered worse under God. Would you like to know about the Blue Mosque?"

They visited the Blue Mosque. They visited Topkapi Palace and the marketplace. The guide urged them into the premises of a rug merchant. They sipped mint tea while the merchant commanded his employees to unroll complicated carpets. The family next door in Antwerp had filled its apartment with such rugs, and Helene somersaulted on them with the little daughter, what was her name, she perished with the rest... This merchant failed to persuade. They left him growling at his lackeys.

A boat slid through liquid lapiz. The wind lifted Angelica's hair. The sun glittered on Toby's mustache. The tour guide nattered on, and then wound up her spiel; and the boat sailed back to the port in silence, passing ruined villas. They disembarked, and Toby tipped the guide. They wandered through winding streets and found a garden café. "Shall we have tea here, Tante Helene?" asked Toby.

She lifted the sleeve of her glove to look at her watch. "You shall have tea here. The hour has come for Madame Guralnik."

"We'll see her too?"

"Ah . . . no. She has scandals to tell me, old Antwerp gossip. The dead are alive to her. But in front of you . . . Regina Guralnik would fall silent." She produced her best twinkle and left them, managing as much of a stride as a small woman could, her black coat swinging, her handbag swinging, her gloved hands in her pockets.

The building she entered could have been found in the poor quarter of any European city—a lobby of chipped tiles, a stairway missing half its wrought iron, an elevator big enough for two thin persons. She noted the details as she had noted them on previous occasions: with severe distaste.

The elevator strained upwards. Its gates creaked open. She walked down a hall and knocked on a door: number Thirty-three.

He opened it.

He had aged a little in the past five years. But his lips were full in his dark face, and his suit was as grave as a diplomat's. He still had the air of a family solicitor. Well, he was a lawyer, wasn't he, whatever other trade he practiced . . . His voice had the deliberate gravity she remembered. She wondered what enterprise his sober firm washed money for these days—guns, girls, drugs, maybe all three.

They seated themselves on either side of a table. They observed a brief silence. Then: "Shall I show you?" she said.

"Please."

She took off her scarf. She took off her gloves. She unzipped a pocket within her handbag and extracted a miniature knife. Laying the left glove flat on the table she picked at the almost invisible stitches attaching a piece of black leather to the palm. Soon only a few remained in place. She raised the glove. The flap she had released hung down. She shook the glove without impatience. Several small diamonds fell onto the table, followed by a large jewel.

It was square cut, and to an untrained eye it might have seemed an emerald, very pale. But these two knew it for the rare thing it was: Papa's green diamond.

It lay between them like a sweetmeat. After several moments the man put a loupe against his eye and picked up the gem and examined it. "Beautiful," he sighed. "Carbon: always hard to believe when you see one like this."

"Yes," she said, resigned to the necessary palaver. "I was brought up on that lesson: the same molecules in our pencils and our fireplaces and the crown jewels. My father wanted us to understand what we were living on . . ."

She saw him again in the dark Antwerp office, her small self curled in his lap. The chartreuse nugget glowed on the mahogany desk. And thirteen years later, in the vault of that Jerusalem bank, the strong stone gleamed in the drawer, gleamed on his palm. "The exact color of your eyes," he said.

The man examined the small diamonds.

"You are holding the remains of my inheritance," she said. "This is my final visit to room Thirty-three."

"You have kept the green beauty for a long time."

She must let it go. The apartment must be maintained, the

wardrobe replenished, the arts patronized, the charities supported. The children's children would keep coming to Jerusalem; she could not allow them to find a straitened old woman. What could you do.

She picked up the jewel. Now *her* hand cradled its power, her skin reflected its lucky color... He named a price, greater than she had expected.

She nodded, briefly unable to speak. She tipped her hand like a ladle; the green ran out. Then: "Please deposit the money in the usual accounts."

"Of course."

Her fingers slid between the buttons of her blouse. She yanked at the cameo; its chain broke. "This goes with the lot," she said, and dropped the thing onto the diamonds.

He glanced down. "Thank you," he said politely.

She gripped the edge of the table, and stood. He stood too. They shook hands.

At the corner a taxi was idling. She curled her fingers to conceal the flapping palm of the glove and then raised her forefinger. The driver had the unwholesome face of the shammas in her girlhood shul, the one who had been caught fondling somebody's child... But he drove peaceably to the hotel. She crossed the lobby quickly; thank God no one was on the elevator to observe her streaked face.

At dinner Toby and Angelica asked for Madame Guralnik.

"She smells of cardamom. It's in every pore, every wrinkle."

At the tables she bet on Thirty-three until her small stake was exhausted.

On the return flight the Rumanians didn't talk at all. They must have lost all the money they came with; they had probably bet their silly earrings and lost them too. *She* had only cheated her country. Greased some syndicate. Disobeyed her father. Thrown away the last of the fortune.

In the cab Helene nestled between Angelica and Toby; beside Toby sat a bearded American. They sped along the highway. They entered Jerusalem. They dropped a passenger on a street off Boulevard Herzl, and Toby remarked that there was no rubbish to be seen. "The Mayor and Sanitation made a deal," said a man in the back seat.

They swerved onto the Jaffa Road. Helene took Toby's hand in her right one and Angelica's in her left. How numb her own hands felt, her arms too. Obediently her relatives turned toward her. They would always turn toward her. But she would slip away from them, wouldn't she . . .

"Tante, your glove is ripped," said Angelica.

. . . like Papa, Mama, the spinster aunts; the girl next door tumbling on the patterned rug, the schnorrers, the naughty shammas; like . . .

She disengaged her hands. Beyond Toby's profile and the profile of the American next to him she saw King George Street, Ben Maimon Street, all the familiar ghostly streets. The cab paused at a traffic light.

In front of an apartment building stood a slope-shouldered form. Its tattered, shiny dress, reflecting the setting sun, cast a greenish glow. Its brown-paper head was topped by an ancient cloche. "The trash collectors missed that creation," said the American.

"The kids who made it must have had fun," said Toby.

"Regina," Helene called. "Regina!"

"Tante . . ." whispered Angelica.

Helene leaned forward, elbowing the bewildered girl. All these years! All these years dealing with thieves in a thievish city. All these years sustaining the weary fable of Salonika, Constantinople, a Turkish husband, a spice shop. Pretending that the goose Guralnik had not stayed in Antwerp. Had not been carted off with the others.

She threw herself across Toby's lap and clutched the American's shoulder. Rapidly she opened the window. She waved her emptied glove again and again at the figure in the ridiculous hat.

The light changed. The cab moved forward. She let go of the American and sank back between Toby and Angelica. She patted their arms with hands that had regained their strength, hands good for a few more years of cleaning house, writing checks, coolly caressing the youngest young visitors. "I'll mend the glove," she promised.

The Message

On a small stone balcony in Jerusalem, across a round glass table, Carolyn was guardedly looking at Terence. Terence was looking at his bowl of yoghurt and apricots; he was not complaining; he was practicing his customary comfortable silence while his mind whirred.

She leaned forward. "I should have bought cereal."

"That's all right." His eyeglasses glinted at her. "The coffee is delicious."

It was Terence's first visit to the city that Carolyn knew well. There was a further imbalance: she spoke serviceable Hebrew, whereas he spoke only English, French, and German, though he read both Latin and Greek. And the weather had made itself his enemy the moment he stepped off the plane. Carolyn knew the weather. She spent every October in Jerusalem, renting the same apartment—it was the pied-à-terre of a Tel Aviv family, complete with two sets of dishes and even two sets of ashtrays—and she always packed for a burst of autumn warmth. This hot Saturday morning her skin caught whatever breeze there was; her arms and throat were bare in a gauzy halter that was almost the same golden brown as her recently dyed hair. But Terence had flown in unexpectedly from a conference on epistemology in Zurich, bringing only his professor's wardrobe. He'd inherited a taste for drab clothing from his Methodist forefathers—their daughter teased that he'd inherited the clothing itself. Last night he'd worn a dark suit and tie to a restaurant where every other male patron had on a short-sleeved shirt buttoning imperfectly over a paunch. He had gone to bed in his underwear—he would have melted in his flannel pajamas—and this morning his face seemed almost as white as his round-necked undershirt. A man with a malady, she'd suddenly thought, her composure sagging. But no: Terence was always pale, just as he was always thin. When they'd met, thirty years ago, he was already slightly stooped.

"I'm used to your hair being gray," he said mildly. "Is this what they call henna?"

She caressed her nape. "Cognac is the official name. In Jerusalem all women of a certain age dye their hair."

"Cognac . . . I didn't know anthropologists could go native."

"Well, no. But I'm not a professional anthropologist." She smiled, trying to lighten the exchange. "I'm not a professional anything; remember?" She had a couple of Master's degrees: certificates but no status. She currently held a grant to study the residents of East Talpiot, one of the oldest Jerusalem suburbs. Once a year she squeezed airfare out of the little grant, and paid a month's rent on this apartment in the leafy Emek Refaim neighborhood. During the other eleven months she lived in Boston with Terence, and taught sociology in an adult center, and wrote a paper or two, and attended a few seminars. "I'm a bronze-crested dilettante," she said now. "Maybe somebody should get a grant to study *me*."

He looked at her with a brief intensity, as if studying her might be a good idea. She knew that look. It meant that he was thinking about Wittgenstein, or maybe Kant.

He had arrived yesterday, Friday. He would leave tomorrow. "The conference is wretched," he'd said over the telephone on Thursday morning. "I'll skip the banquet, come spend the weekend with you. If my arrival won't be an inconvenience," he'd added, not ironic, merely considerate.

It would be a great inconvenience. "Wonderful!" Carolyn had said to Terence, south warming north, wife deceiving husband, Mediterranean splashing onto Swiss shrubbery. "I'll meet you at the airport."

"Not necessary."

"The cabbies would skin you. I'll be there!"

Then she'd had to climb the stone stairs, to knock on Natan's door, to explain the situation, to endure his immediate fury.

"Twenty-eight days a year we have together; and now you rob me of three of them!" He held her by the forearms and shook her slightly. "And Saturday night, we have tickets for the quartet!" he remembered.

"I'm sorry," she said. What a bellow! *"You* go to the concert."

"Alone? Bite your tongue! You are *sans merci,* like all lovely women. Without compassion. *L'lo rachmim!"* he wound up, though he usually spoke Hebrew to her only when within earshot of American tourists. "Carolyn?" he then inquired, signaling the end of his outburst.

She was silent.

"Oh, your Christian tolerance," he sighed. "A Jewish woman would have already told me to shut up. I'll visit my daughter this weekend. I haven't been to Haifa for three months. I'll play with my granddaughter. Little Miriam is a beauty, too. Okay?"

He scowled at her and then grinned. Gold flashed from the brownish mouth that always smelled of tobacco, though he smoked only five cigarettes a day in her presence, numbering each one aloud. She figured that he consumed fifteen or twenty when she was out conducting interviews. Their aroma had seeped into her apartment. Luckily she found it aphrodisiac.

He was tall, wide, big-bellied, large-freckled; a teacher of high-school biology, retired. His apartment, up one flight and across the hall, was a mirror image of hers. Since his wife's death six years ago he had turned the place into a kind of terrarium. Mushrooms flourished underneath panes of dark glass. Thistles dried on a loveseat. Vines, climbing up strings, completely enclosed the balcony. Sometimes Natan and Carolyn made love within this green tabernacle, lying on an old mattress pad. The morning sun, penetrating here and there, further mottled his piebald back.

Her balcony—the balcony of the Zebelons of Tel Aviv—betrayed its owners' indifference to horticulture. A single orange tree grew crookedly out of a tub. In the center of the table Carolyn kept daisies in a jar. Across the homely bouquet she and Terence now made their plans. They would return to the Old City, would continue through its labyrinth. Yesterday at one of the stalls she'd bought Terence a loose woven collarless shirt striped in purple and orange; he'd smiled and named it The Garment. He had walked contentedly beside her; in his usual attentive silence he had observed alleys, excavations, beggars, and corners golden with ancient dust.

Now he studied the city map. "This afternoon let's visit the University. We can take bus number Four."

"If we don't mind waiting for it all day. The busses don't run on Shabbat, not while the sun is up. But about an hour into the darkness they move again, glowing, all of them at once, like night-blooming plants..."

The telephone rang. It rang again. Terence raised his eyebrows.

"I've got a machine," she told him.

The instrument was nearby. Her own voice floated onto the balcony, first reciting practiced Hebrew, then English. "...return your call as soon as possible."

The caller was a breathless American hanger-on, everybody knew her, everybody avoided her. "I haven't even laid eyes on you this visit," she wailed into the void. "Please get in touch."

Carolyn, smiling at Terence, turned her thumb down like an Emperor.

"Do taxis run on the Sabbath?" he asked.

"They do; and..."

The telephone again. This time the caller was one of her Yemenites from East Talpiot. The woman's Hebrew was accented but clear. *"Madame, I cannot meet with you on Wednesday; my son returns from Army. Maybe Thursday? At ten in the morning?"*

Carolyn nodded, as if the woman could see her.

"Your appointment with the hairdresser is changed," said Terence. "From one day—I heard *yom;* that's day, isn't it?—to another *yom.*"

149

"Almost! It was an interviewee; but you're right about the switch in day. What an ear you've got. A month here and you'd be bargaining with the *moniot*—the taxis..."

A third ring. "I've received more calls this morning than all last week," Carolyn said. "My friends are putting on a show for you," she added, her real voice intertwining with her recorded one, though they were both real, weren't they; the difference was temporal, not essential...

Natan. The caller was Natan. Natan the mischievous, Natan the yea-sayer. He spoke in the Hebrew tongue, in case Terence was listening. He spoke in the vocabulary of an acquaintance, in case someone else was listening. His tone was perhaps too rich. But the message was unimpeachable.

"Carolyn, this is your pal Natan. I have come to Haifa to visit my granddaughter. We have bathed three times already—the bouyancy of the sea has made me young again. In the blue depths I thought of my green balcony, and I call to ask you to water the vines on my behalf. I will return on Monday. Monday."

She had inclined her head slightly at the first sound of his voice. She was afraid to straighten it, as if the gesture might give her away.

"Another *yom*," said Terence.

"Yom sheni. Monday," said Carolyn; and now she dared resettle her head on her neck. "My upstairs neighbor is in Haifa visiting his family; he asks me to water his plants."

"You are not telling the truth."

"...pardon?"

"Forgive me; you are not rendering the message faithfully."

Carolyn closed her eyes. "He mentioned swimming with his

150

granddaughter. It was rejuvenating. I believe that was all he said, except for naming his day of return. The sea is blue, he said."

"He said your eyes are blue," said Terence.

She opened them now; but his gaze was elsewhere, resting on the little telephone table just inside the archway. His lips pursed with distaste. "I will tell you what he said, your friend, Mr. Etan..."

"Natan," she helplessly corrected.

"...Mr. Natan, he said that your eyes, though not as blue as the sea, though green, really, have spokes of a darker color." His voice labored, as if he really were translating. "Your eyes remind him of a tropical leaf."

"He didn't say that, any of that, Terence, honestly, what are you imagining..."

He continued to stare at the telephone and its attachment. "He said that when his arms are encircling your naked back he thinks he is touching silk." He paused to hunch and then widen his shoulders as if trying to wriggle out of a jacket; Carolyn longed to help him, but there was no jacket. "The small rough mole on your collarbone makes his blood pound. He yearns to fall into your lap, to lick your salty belly."

In all their years together Terence had never spoken to her in such a manner. Once or twice he had admired a piece of jewelry; and he had often thanked her for her graciousness to the junior faculty. Otherwise they spoke of his work, her work, their children; friends; books. Their lovemaking was conducted in peaceable silence. Silence made guilt endurable.

"He yearns to hear you laugh," said Terence to the answering machine. "He finds it thrilling. He thinks he cannot live without your voice. He thinks he cannot live without your presence . . . without you."

Again, the familiar silence. Carolyn considered rising from her chair, kneeling before her husband, acknowledging the declaration that she recognized as his own, the avowal that had been wrung from him as if by thumbscrews. But no; melodrama would shame him; and besides, if she got up she might fall. Her trembling hands rummaged through her new hair; her wrists crossed in front of her breasts; finally her splayed fingers came to rest on the table. Still seated, she watched his profile. Two drops of sweat slowly made their way down the side of his neck. When the second had spent itself on his undershirt she said in a low tone, "My final round of interviews is nearly over. The research is finished. I'll be coming home in November for good."

He flushed purple, as if enduring a merciless spasm. Then his normal pallor returned. He wiped his mouth with his napkin and looked at his watch. "Shall we be on our way?" And left the balcony.

"Put on The Garment," she called after him.

But when he came out of the bedroom he was wearing one of his usual white shirts.

If Love Were All

I.

"Before you came here—what did you do?" Mrs. Levinger asked during Sonya's first month in London.

"Books."

"Wrote?"

"Kept."

"Well, then. Think of this enterprise as a balance sheet. On balance the children are better off. Don't you have a handkerchief, Sonya? Take mine."

The sort of incident that triggered this exchange—the removal of a child from his cohort by medical personnel—would occur frequently, but Sonya had just witnessed it for the first time: the kindly faces of doctor and nurse; the impassivity of the other children, imperfectly concealing their panic. Many wore cardboard

153

placards, like Broadway sandwich men. LONDON, LONDRES, LOND, ENGLAND, the boards variously said.

"There is something a little wrong with your chest," the doctor had told the child, in German.

"We will make it well," said the nurse, in French.

The little boy spoke only Polish and Yiddish. He spoke them one after the other as he was led away. Then he screamed them, one after the other, stiffening his legs so as not to walk. "Mama!" he called as he was lifted up, though his mother was no doubt dead. "Big sister!" he cried as he was carried off, though his big sister, a girl of eight, had fallen to the floor.

"You will get used to it," said Mrs. Levinger to Sonya. "Oh, dear."

Sonya was an American in town for the War. For several summers in the recent past she had led a gypsy life on the Rhode Island coast—danced on the beach, shared a one-room house with an ageing tenor who loved her to distraction. These facts were a matter of indifference to Mrs. Levinger and the rest of beseiged London . . . or would have been a matter of indifference if Sonya had broadcast her history. But she said little about herself. When, during the previous year, friends in Providence (her home during the three seasons that weren't summer) begged to know why she was going abroad, throwing up her jobs (she taught Hebrew at Sunday School and she kept accounts for various small enterprises) . . . when people posed these questions, Sonya answered, "Because of the hurricane."

Her beach house had four slanted walls and an uncertain roof. No electricity, no running water. The hurricane of 1938 lifted the place from its cement foundation and spun off with it. Not a stick of Sonya's belongings was ever recovered—not the woodburning stove, the chemical toilet, the teapot, the garments hanging on hooks. In the weeks that followed the storm she sat in her hillside Providence apartment and stared at the center of town, also ravaged but gradually repairing itself. But her own life would not be repaired; she was already sliding into unrelieved respectability. Somebody would sooner or later ask her to marry him—despite middle age, despite lack of beauty, somebody sometimes did. The tenor had already proposed. She feared that, no longer buoyed by her annual summer of freedom, she would weakly say yes.

So she had offered herself instead to the American Joint Distribution Committee, affectionately called the Joint. She went to New York for an interview. The interviewer, an overweight man in shirt sleeves and a rumpled vest, said, "Good that you speak Hebrew."

"I don't, you know," Sonya told him. "I have enough Biblical Hebrew to teach classes Aleph and Beth."

"If you are sent to Palestine your Hebrew will improve," he said. And, glancing down at her dossier: "You speak French."

"I studied French in high school, that's what it says. Once, in Quebec, I ordered a glass of wine. And Yiddish—I haven't used it in decades."

Their eyes met. "The situation in Europe is desperate," he said. "One thousand Polish-German Jews have been expelled by Germany and refused by Poland and are starving and freezing and dying of dysentery in a no-man's land between the two countries. Many are children. Several organizations are working together to help—and working together is not, I see you studied Latin as well, our normal *modus operandi*. Two Jews, three opinions, I'm sure you understand." He checked his flow with a visible effort. His mouth opened and closed several times but he managed not to speak.

155

"I'll do any job," she said in this interval. "I just don't want you to count on languages."

"Do you sing? We find people who sing are comfortable in our work."

"I am moderately musical." Very moderately. She thought of the tenor. She could still say Yes. But she did not want to become a caretaker.

The fat man's gaze loosened at last. He looked out the window. "All agencies are working together to get these people from Zbaszyn into England. For this, for all our efforts, we need staff members who are efficient and unsentimental. Languages are of secondary importance. The Joint trusts my judgment."

She signed a sort of contract. Then she said, "You should know, I am occasionally sentimental."

A smile, or something like it, landed on his large face and immediately scurried off. She suspected that, like many fat men, he danced well.

Sonya took the train back to Providence. After several months she learned that she would be sent to London and there loaned to another Organization, one helping refugee children. Then came a steamer ticket. Rapidly she put the books of her clients into order, and stored her furniture, and gave herself a good-bye party in the emptied apartment. She took the train again and in New York boarded a ship bound for Southampton. The fat man showed up to say good-bye, carrying a spray of gladiolas.

"How kind," she said, trying not to shudder at the funereal flowers.

"It is not the usual procedure," he admitted.

By the time Sonya arrived at the London office the displaced Polish-Germans were already rescued or lost. But War had been declared. There was plenty of work to be done.

The Joint found her a bed-sitter in Camden Town. The landlady and her family lived on the ground floor; otherwise the place was home to unattached people. Each room had a gas fire and a cooker. It took Sonya a while to get used to the smells. She had to get used to footsteps, too—there was no carpet, and everyone on the upper floors traveled past Sonya's room. There was an old lady with twittering feet. "My dear," she said whenever she saw Sonya. A large man looked at her with yellow-eyed interest. His slow footsteps sounded like pancakes dropped from a height. An elderly man lightly marched. With his impressive bearing and his white mustache he resembled an ambassador, but he was the proprietor of the neighborhood newsstand. Two secretaries tripped out together every morning after curling their hair with tongs. The first time Sonya smelled singed hair she thought the house was on fire. And there was a lame man of about forty, their only foreigner. Sonya didn't count herself as foreign; she was an American cousin. But the lame man—he had a German accent.

He had dark skin and bad teeth. Eyebrows sheltered glowing brown eyes—eyes that seemed to be reflecting a fire even when they were merely glancing at envelopes on the hall table. His legs were of differing lengths—that accounted for the limp. Sonya recognized his limping progress whenever he came up or down the staircase: ONE pause Two, ONE pause Two; and whenever he passed her door: ONE Two, ONE Two, ONE Two.

157

The children came, wave after wave of them. Polish children, Austrian children, Hungarian children, German children. Some came like parcels bought from the governments who withheld passports from their parents. These children wore coats, and each carried a satchel. Some came in unruly bands, having lived like squirrels in the mountains or like rats by the rivers. Some came escorted by social workers who couldn't wait to get rid of them. Few understood English. Some knew only Yiddish. Some had infectious diseases. Some seemed feebleminded; but it turned out that they had been only temporarily enfeebled by hardship.

They slept for a night or two in a seedy hotel near the Waterloo station. Sonya and Mrs. Levinger, who directed the Agency, stayed in the hotel too, intending to sleep—they were always tired, for the bombing had begun. But the women failed to sleep, for the children—not crying; they rarely cried—wandered through the halls, or hid in closets smoking cigarettes, or went up and down the lift. The next day, or the next day but one, Sonya and Mrs. Levinger escorted them to their quarters in the countryside, and deposited them with stout farm families, these Viennese who had never seen a cow; or left them in hastily assembled orphanages staffed with elderly schoolteachers, these Berliners who had known only the tender hands of nursemaids; or stashed them in a Bishop's Palace, these Polish children for whom Christians were the devil. The Viennese kids might have found the Palace suitable; the Hungarians would have formed a vigorous troupe within the orphanage; the little Poles, familiar with chickens, might have become comfortable on the farms. But the billets rarely matched the children. The Organization took what it could get. After the children were settled, however uneasily, Sonya and Mrs. Levinger rode the train back to London, Mrs. Levinger returning to her husband and Sonya to solitude.

For months she nodded at the dark man and he nodded at her.

They said Good Evening.

One day they left the house at the same time, and walked together to the Underground.

He lived two floors above her, he said. She already knew that from her attention to footsteps.

His room contained an upright piano left behind by a previous tenant. He managed to keep it in tune. "A piano is so rare in furnished...digs," he said, seeming to relish the British word.

He was on his way to give piano lessons. His pupils were London children whose parents thus far refused to evacuate them. She was on her way to her office. He left the Tube first. "I hope we meet again, Miss..."

"Sofrankovitch," she said. She didn't tell him that the honorific was properly 'Mrs.' Her childless marriage had ended long ago.

After that, as if the clock previously governing their lives had been exchanged for a different timepiece, they ran into each other often. They met on the narrow winding High Street. They bought newspapers at the kiosk manned by their distinguished looking housemate. They queued at the greengrocer's, each leaving with a few damaged apples. They found themselves together at the fishmonger's. Both were partial to smoked fish, willing to exchange ration coupons for the luxury.

Often, at night, after he came home from work, after she came home, they sat by her gas fire.

"Providence," he mused. "And the place of the hurricane?"

"Narragansett."

"Naghaghansett," he rolled out, his vowels aristocratically long, his consonants irreparably guttural.

"Something like that," she smiled into the shadows.

Eugene had never visited the United States, though as a young man he had studied piano in Paris. "Yes, I heard Boulanger." Except for that heady time he had not left Germany until three years earlier when one of the other refugee Agencies helped him emigrate to London. Still short of forty then, his parents dead, his sister safely married in Shanghai, his ability to make a living secure—he was one of the easy repatriation cases, she supposed.

His father, he told her, had fought for the Kaiser.

She had been a young woman during that War. Yes, she knew that Germany had once been good to its Jews, its Jews faithful to their rulers.

He stretched his long, unmatched legs toward the meager blue flames. "I'm glad we met."

One noontime—*mirabile dictu,* the New York fat man might have said—they ran into each other far from home, in Kensington Gardens.

"I am attending a concert," Eugene said. "Come with me."

"My lunch break... not much time."

"The performers also are on lunch break. You won't be late. You won't be very late," he corrected, with his usual slight pedantry.

They hurried along the streets leading toward the river, passing bomb craters, and passing shelters of brick, of cement, of corrugated iron. Their own shelter back in Camden Town was an underground bunker, a crypt, safer than these. But it trembled, sometimes, and then little children cried, and women paled, and men too. Sonya soothed whichever toddler crawled into her lap, and smiled encouragement at the child's mother. It was hard to breathe. Suppose the thing should cave in—they would all suffocate. Being struck above ground, being blasted, being shattered into a thousand pieces like her beach house, that would be better than not breathing... There were times she did not go into the shelter at all, but stayed sitting on the floor in her blacked-out room, arms around shins. Behind her on the windowsill bloomed a sturdy geranium, red in the daytime, purple in this almost blindness. And if the house should be hit, and if she should be found amidst its shattered moldings and heaps of glass and smoking bricks, her head at an odd angle, her burned hair as black as it had been in her youth... if she should be found in the rubble, people would think, if they thought anything at all, that she had slept through the siren. She might have taken a bit too much, the wineshop keeper would say to his wife—he no doubt guessed that his customer sometimes sacrificed food for whisky. She was working so very hard, Mrs. Levinger would remark.

Eugene led her to a church. Sonya looked up at the organ loft. A few parishioners on their own lunch breaks settled into the empty pews. One slowly lowered his forehead onto the back of the pew in front of him, then lifted it, then lowered it again.

Downstairs, in a small chapel, a dozen people waited on chairs and two performers waited on a platform. The standing young man held a viola by its neck. The young woman sat at a piano, head bowed as if awaiting execution. A note on the mimeographed program mentioned that these twenty-year-old twins had recently

161

arrived from Czechoslovakia. The performance began. The sister played with precision. Eugene's fingers played along with her, on his own thighs. The brother made love to his instrument. In the intervals between selections the attentive audience was entertained by faint sounds of organ practice from above. The concert lasted less than an hour. When the twins and their guests filed upstairs, Sonya looked for the parishioner who had banged his forehead against the pew-back, but he was gone.

As Eugene had promised, Sonya was not very late getting back to work. Still, Mrs. Levinger had already returned from lunch. She was on the telephone. She gave Sonya a distracted nod and hung up.

"The next batch is here," she said. "The French ones."

The usual setup: at one end of a large function room volunteers stood at bridge tables; at the other end a trestle table holding loaves of bread, and biscuits, and plates of sausages, and jugs of milk.

Forty children who had been fending for themselves for six months now huddled in the middle of the room as if, were they to approach the food, they would be shot.

One girl's hair was the color of lamplight.

Mrs. Levinger hoisted herself onto a folding chair and grasped its back for a moment while her rump threatened to topple her. Then she stood up. Once standing she did not falter or shake.

Sonya made note of various details—it was part of her job. There was a small pale fellow who looked sick, but the doctors hadn't detained him. Hunger and fatigue, probably. Two little girls gripped each others' hands. Many children carried smaller children.

The fair-haired girl carried an instrument case.

Mrs. Levinger welcomed them in French. They were being sent

to villages in the Cotswolds, she said. Hills, she elaborated. They could keep their belongings. Siblings would not be separated. The host families would not be Jewish. But they would be sympathetic.

"I am not Jewish either," said a dark boy.

"Ah, Pierre," reproved a bigger boy. "It's all right, in this place."

The children made their slow silent way to the trestle table. Soon all were eating—all except the tall blonde girl with the instrument. She seemed about to approach Mrs. Levinger. But it was a feint. She swerved toward Sonya. "Madame..."

"*Oui,*" said Sonya. "*Voulez vous...*"

"I speak English." Her eyes were gray. She had a straight nose, a curly mouth, a small chin. "I do not wish to go into the countryside."

"What is your name?"

"Lotte," with a shrug, as if any name would do. "I am from Paris. I wish to stay in London."

"Your instrument..."

"A violin," said Lotte. "I tried to sell it when we ran out of food in Marseilles, but no one wanted to buy it. I am skilled, Madame. I can play in an orchestra. Or in a café—gypsy music."

"I wish," Sonya began. "I cannot," she tried again. "There is no arrangement in London for refugee children," she finally said. "Only in the villages."

"I am no child. I am seventeen."

Sonya shook her head.

The lids dropped. "Sixteen. Truly, Madame."

"Call me Sonya."

"*Merci.* Madame Sonya, I am sixteen next month, if I had my papers I could prove it, but my papers were lost, everything was

163

lost, even the photographs of my father, only the violin..." Lotte swallowed. "I will be sixteen in three weeks. Please believe me."

"I do." Mrs. Levinger was glancing at them; other children needed attention. "You must go to the Cotswolds now. I'll try to make some better arrangement."

Lotte said, "Empty words," and turned away.

"No!" Was she always to be denied sentiment, must she be only efficient forever?—she who was moderately musical. "I love gypsy tunes," she said. "Look, this is my address," scribbling on some brown paper; "Look, I will try to find you a café, or maybe a..."

Lotte took the paper. Sonya's last sight of her was on the train, a different train from the one Sonya was taking. Lotte was standing in the aisle, clasping the violin to her thin chest.

"I would like to give you a ring," Eugene said.

"Oh!"

"I may be interned."

"It won't happen," fervently. But it was happening every day. Aliens suspected of being spies—Jews among them—were shut up in yellow prisons.

Eugene said, "My other suit, my piano scores—they can fend for themselves. But my mother's ring—I owe it respect. It eluded German customs, it eluded also my own conscience."

She glanced at him. In the light of the gas fire his skin looked as dark as the geranium.

"I should have sold it to repay my rescuers," he explained. "But it is only a little diamond. And it meant much to my mother."

"Ah...your father gave it to her."

"Her lover gave it to her. My mother was born in Lyon; in

164

Berlin she retained her French attitude toward marriage. And then, of course, my father was so much older."

"Older?" A dozen years separated Sonya and Eugene—she had recently turned fifty-two without mentioning it.

"Twenty years older." Eugene fished in his pocket. Something twinkled. He put it into her palm.

Two weeks afterwards he was taken away.

II.

By the beginning of Sonya's second year in London she had acquired women friends and men friends and a favorite tearoom and two favorite pubs and several favorite walks. She had adopted the style of the women around her—cotton dresses, low-heeled shoes—but she spurned the brave little hats. She swept her gray hair back from her brow and pinned barrettes behind her ears. Her hair curved like annoyed feathers below the barrettes.

She knew where to get necessaries on the black market. Occasionally, for her small clients, she used that knowledge. Sometimes she used it for herself—a bottle of contraband cognac was stashed at the bottom of her armoire waiting for Eugene's return.

She went to lectures in drafty halls. She went to briefings with people who had recently returned from Vichy and Salonika and Haifa. She went to patched-together concert operas and to stunning theatricals—once, in a theater, she heard Laurence Olivier's voice rise above the sound of bombs.

She attended exhibitions of new watercolors. A few times, during the summer, she bathed at Brighton. "You must play!" ordered Mrs. Levinger. She received letters from friends in Rhode Island and her aunt in Chicago and the fat man in New York and the tenor and Eugene. She kept track of that first tubercular boy, visited him in his seaside sanatorium. The Yiddish of her childhood stirred during the early visits; but after a few months she discovered that new words were sticking to him like burrs. Soon they spoke only English. Together they watched the slate-colored sea. Sitting next to his little chaise, his translucent hand in hers, she told him about the hurricane that had sliced her own life in two. "A tall wave smashed onto our cove."

"A hill of water," he experimented.

"Yes, yes! A mountain."

She kept in touch with the sister, too, in her berth in a cottage. A year after the boy was taken away Sonya and Mrs. Levinger presided over the reunion of the children, the girl rosy, the boy pale but free of disease. The foster mother agreed to take him too. "For she pines, she does," said that kindly soul.

"Of course you remember Roland Rosenberg," Mrs. Levinger said.

"Of course." They shook hands. He was a little less fat, but it would be tactless to say so. They spoke of work in a unnecessary way—it was as if she knew by heart the papers in his shapeless briefcase, as if he could trace each line on her face back to the situation that had drawn it there. But they did talk, some, in a gloomy restaurant. His table manners were terrible. His handkerchief was a disgrace. His peculiar smile recurred now and again—upturned lips, a look of wonder. Mark Twain, he told her, was a passion with him. Some day he wanted to follow Twain's journey around the world.

"And the composers you like?" she idly asked.

"Franz Lehar is my favorite."

Lehar: beloved by Hitler. "Oh, dear," said Sonya.

"Shameful, isn't it. The Joint should fire me."

There was no cab. When was there ever a cab? He walked her home. "I will be back some day."

"Good." Good? What were they doing to Eugene?

"The *New York Times,* please," she said one evening, and took the paper from the distinguished gentleman. Standing at the kiosk, she looked at the front page. The War occupied most of it, though there were City scandals too. The Dakotas were suffering a drought. She folded the paper under her arm—she would read it by lamplight, at home; there were no air raids nowadays.

From his recess he rumbled: "How are you, Miss Sofrankovitch?"

She turned back. "... Okay, thanks."

"I have newspapers from Belgrade today, a rare event."

"Ah, I don't read Yugoslavian."

"No? You read French, perhaps. I have ..."

"Not really; and not German either," she anticipated. "I can read elementary Hebrew, Mr. ...."

"Smith."

"Smith." She peered at him, and at the darkness behind him. "My own parents sold newspapers," she confided.

167

"Indeed."

"Yes, in a store. They sold cigarettes also, candies, notions. Notions; an Americanism; perhaps you are not familiar with it."

"Haven't a notion!" He turned his attention to the next customer. Business first, of course; but how urgently Sonya now wanted to describe to him that small round couple, her parents, that pair of innocents to whom she had been born long after they had given up the idea of family. By then the store itself was their issue—a close, warm cave. In it she grew into a tall girl; graduated from high school, from Normal school; from it she married a handsome and untrustworthy boy. She kept the marriage going and the store too until both parents were safely dead.

Mr. Smith disposed of his customer. Sonya leaned across the shelf of newspapers. The interior, big enough for two if the two were disposed to be friendly, was adorned with magazines clipped to bare boards, and advertisements for beer. The place was redolent of tobacco, the fragrance of her childhood. Eugene's bad teeth were made browner still by his cigarette habit. She inhaled. "I sold the place during the Depression," she told Mr. Smith. He leaned against a poster: *Loose Lips Lose Lives.* She withdrew her upper body from the booth and again stood erect, continuing her history. "I sold the living quarters too. I rented an apartment and also bought a . . . house, a house on the shore, it was destroyed by the hurricane, but perhaps here you didn't know of the hurricane."

"Oh, we knew of it. We saw photographs. *Comment donc!*" he said, turning to another patron who must be familiar, a little Frenchman in a floorwalker's frock coat and polished shoes.

Sonya turned away and walked up the High Street toward home.

Home? A wallpapered room with a gas fire. A round table and turn-up bed and desk and armchair and radio and lamp and battered armoire. A little locked jewel box in which reposed her mother's wedding ring; the silk handkerchief from the tenor which he himself had received from a famous mezzo; Eugene's diamond. Yes, home. Her home was wherever she was. "You have no nesting instinct," her husband accused when he was leaving. "Lucky for us we never had a child. You would have kept it in a bureau drawer."

No mail for her. Up the stairs, then. She boiled two eggs on the cooker and put a slice of bread on the toasting fork. She had no butter and no jam but she did have a glass and a half of wine in yesterday's bottle, and she uncorked it gratefully. She read the paper during this repast, saving the obituaries for last, nice little novelettes, it was unlikely that she'd ever recognize anybody on that page until Rolypoly Rosenberg burst a blood vessel; no, really, he wasn't the apoplectic type, and he was losing weight anyway... she read of the tenor's death.

He had collapsed while singing to a large audience of soldiers at Fort Devens. He was seventy-three. His career had spanned six decades. He had sung all the great roles, though never at the Met. His radio program was popular during the thirties. Its signature song was "The Story of a Starry Night." He left three daughters and eight grandchildren.

There had been only seven grandchildren when she left; otherwise she could have written the obituary herself.

That night she wept for him. Of course she had been wise not to join her destiny to his. She was not meant for the settled life—not she, not Sonya, not this human leaf that had appeared unexpectedly in an overheated notions store and gotten popped as it were into a jelly glass by the proud but bewildered storekeepers. Oh, they had loved her, Mama and Papa; and she had loved them; and she had loved her husband for a while; and some others after him; and she had loved the tenor, too. But her love was airy, not earthbound; and so she could be scooped up like a handful of chickweed by Roland Rosenberg and flung onto the stones of London, there to send out shallow creepers into this borough, that block of flats, the derelict basement over by the river. The children. Sleeplessly she counted them. Some were in the city now. There were two small boys living with a mother who had become deranged when the oldest son was shot dead at the border; those tykes took care of her. There was a family with a dimwitted daughter who herself had borne a dimwitted daughter. "That shouldn't happen; children tend toward the mean!" Sonya objected, as if statistical epidemiology would acknowledge the error and revise the little girl's intelligence. Mrs. Levinger ignored her outburst. There were teenaged girls from Munich working as waitresses who refused to confide in Sonya though they allowed her to buy them dinner. And...

The scratching at the door could have been a small animal. Had it been preceded by footsteps? Sonya was out of bed immediately, her left hand on the bolt, her right on the knob. Was that the smell of cigarettes? She opened the door.

Lotte stepped across the threshold. Her eyes swiveled from corner to corner. She saw the round table and laid her violin carefully under it. Then she turned, and fell into Sonya's arms.

They feasted on bacon in the morning. Lotte had carried it from the farm. Sonya fried it along with a hoarded tomato, and toasted her last two pieces of bread. They dipped the toast into the grease.

170

"Now we have to talk," Sonya said when they had wiped their fingers on her only napkin. Lotte's fingers were more deliberate than delicate—rather like Eugene's at the piano.

"The family," Lotte began. "They were kind. The church organist befriended me. There was a boy at school, too: an English boy, I mean," and Sonya knew what she meant—the local boy's attention supplemented but didn't supplant the calf-love of the immigrant boys already attached to her. Such an enchanting sweep of lash.

"The family," Sonya prompted.

"I left a letter. Don't send me back. Let me stay here with you."

It was against the Organization's rules. But the Organization's rules often got ignored. South of the river five teenaged boys from Bucharest lived in one room, supporting themselves who knew how, though pickpocketing was suspected. Sometimes Mrs. Levinger hauled them in. "It's not good for the Jews, what you're doing." The boys looked at their feet.

"They endanger our enterprise," Mrs. Levinger said later to Sonya.

"A couple of them actually work as plasterers."

"Well, we do need plasterers," said Mrs. Levinger, deflected.

"Rumor has it that they steal only from rich drunks."

"Rumor! Rumor has it that Winston is planning an invasion. I'll believe that when it happens. We're probably going to be invaded"; and Sonya imagined Mrs. Levinger picking up the fireplace shovel and banging the heads of Germans foolish enough to enter her office.

Meanwhile the young Rumanians lifted wallets in Mayfair. And an unlicensed pair of Polish doctors kept an unlicensed clinic in

171

Clapham Commons. Belgians who had arrived with diamonds in their hems sold those diamonds on the black market and decamped for South America, bestowing not one shilling to the Agency that had brought them to London, a different Agency, but still. "Not against the rules," mentioned Mrs. Levinger. "Not *comme il faut,* however." Sonya thought of Eugene's mother's little stone.

"I'll sleep on the floor," Lotte was saying. "I'll get a job. I'll pay my share. You'll see."

"What's this about a French girl," said Mrs. Levinger a few days later. "I had a letter from a family..."

"She's with me."

They exchanged a steady look. "We can manage a small allowance," said Mrs. Levinger.

"If that becomes necessary," said Sonya—in a rather cold voice, since she was almost in tears—"I will let you know."

It did not become necessary. On Saturday Lotte asked Sonya for a few shillings; also, could Sonya borrow a screwdriver from someone in the building? Well, she'd try. Mr. Smith was at his kiosk. The twittering old lady had gone to live with her daughter. The yellow-eyed man was out. Eugene was of course not in. Sonya finally knocked on the secretaries' door, expecting no luck. But the secretaries owned an entire tool chest; they'd built a hutch for their window. They were raising generations of rabbits. "How... sweet," said Sonya.

"Cash," explained one of the young women. "The nobs still love their *lapin.*"

Sonya came downstairs with the screwdriver to find Lotte returning from the High Street with a brass lock and two keys.

Within an hour she had affixed it to the door of the armoire. Then she stowed her violin next to the cognac. She locked the closet. For a moment she sank into the chair. "Safe," she sighed. Sonya forebore to mention the bombings; perhaps they wouldn't start again.

Returning the screwdriver, Sonya ran into the landlady. "I have a...guest."

"I noticed, dearie. I'll have to charge a bit more."

Every day Lotte went out looking for work. She came back disappointed. At night they went to concerts. It was like having Eugene back. "At Saint Aidan's—there's a choir singing tonight," Lotte would say; or "A *basso* over at Marylebone—just got here from there." Scattered musicians formed makeshift ensembles. "How did you hear about this?" asked Sonya as they drifted home from a trio.

"I went to a music store looking for a job...met some other string players..."

Lotte began to play on street corners. Sonya warned her to watch for policemen. At first she played in outer London. But though small bands of admirers collected (she reported matter-of-factly to Sonya), too few coins fell into the open case at her feet. She moved toward the center of town. She played in Picadilly; in the Strand; near Whitehall. "I saw Churchill," she exclaimed. Everyone knew that Churchill was directing the War from underground offices; but there were rumors of lookalike doubles, hundreds of them, deployed to fool the enemy and maybe the populace.

In Lotte's new sites she collected enough money to meet the landlady's rise in rent, to buy cheese and smoked fish and peaches, to insist that Sonya always take the greater share. "You are my patron, my benefactor, my angel."

"I repudiate those roles. This peach is heavenly."

"My mother, then . . . no, no, you are too young."

". . . hardly too young."

"Big sister!"

Sonya was still on loan to Mrs. Levinger from the Joint; but Mrs. Levinger's mandate had altered. Few refugees managed to get in now, but there was plenty to do for the ones already here. Families were starving. Sonya made rounds with ration books, with money, sometimes with piecework from factories—she might have been a foreman sweating workers. Lotte fiddled for coins.

One spring evening Sonya decided to cross the river before going home. No raids for a long time now, just a few planes every so often, scared off by the ack-ack guns. On the embankment she saw a clown . . . no, it wasn't a clown, it was a girl. Yes, it was a clown: Lotte.

She was near a bombed-out site beginning to be rebuilt. Those plasterers—were the Rumanian boys among them? Lotte wore wide plaid trousers underneath her usual skimpy jacket. She had found a diplomat's homburg—snatched it, maybe—and she had blacked the space between her upper teeth and darkened some of her freckles. Her pale hair foamed beneath the hat. She played the street repertoire that she practiced at home—Kreisler, Smetana, Dvorak—with exaggerated melancholy and exaggerated vivacity. "To make their eyes water," she'd explained. "To give them a swooping finale."

After the swooping finale she walked among the loiterers, her hat upside down in her hand. When she came to Sonya she bowed. Teasingly she shook the hat. Sonya reached into the pocket of her raincoat but Lotte moved on.

The listeners drifted away. A smiling Lotte returned to Sonya. "Let's feast!"

"Those clothes!" Sonya smiled back.

The homburg turned out to be a trick hat, collapsible. Lotte shed the wide trousers with one twist of her nimble hips, revealing a pleated skirt, one of the two she owned. With trousers and hat in one hand and the violin in the other she led the way to a pub.

They sat in a corner booth, the two of them—three, counting the instrument. Lamplight streamed through stained-glass windows into the noisy place.

"I did well today," said Lotte handing the money to Sonya, who knew better than to refuse. "But I would prefer a steadier income."

"You should be at school," Sonya moaned.

"Soon I will find a place in an orchestra. Or a nightclub."

Sonya ordered a second whisky.

Roland Rosenberg appeared the next week and stayed for forty-eight hours. Though still fat he was thinner and worn. But: "You are losing weight, Sonya Sofrankovitch," he had the nerve to say. "Take care of yourself."

And then—Lotte's mad dreams came true. A restaurant keeper heard her, hired her, provided crepe trousers and a sequinned jacket. Café Bohemia was a hodgepodge of banquettes, murals, gilt, and salvage. Sonya dropped in one or two nights a week.

There were no more eye-watering swoops, no more glittering glissandos. She played Brahms, Liszt, Mendelssohn. She looked twice her age, Sonya thought. But then Sonya herself probably looked twice hers.

And Lotte found a trio—two old men and one old woman—who wanted a second violinist. "They play very well," Lotte commended, "though none of them is Jewish." The recitals were free; but the performers were paid, sometimes, by a Foundation in Canada. Lotte had to rifle the account she shared with Sonya to buy a blue dress with a collar—the sequinned outfit was not considered appropriate.

She had every right to rifle the account. She was contributing more than Sonya. She bought a fold-up cot and no longer had to sleep on the floor. She bought a second geranium. She bought whisky, though she herself drank only an occasional glass of wine. And when Sonya turned fifty-three, Lotte bought a pair of train tickets; and they journeyed to Penzance for a weekend, and stayed in a hotel, and walked on the beach, holding hands like sisters.

ONE and Two. ONE and Two.

A Sunday afternoon. Lotte was out playing with the quartet.

ONE Two ONE Two.

Sonya opened her door. This time it was he.

"The war has gone on so long it seems like peace," Sonya wrote to her aunt. "One day is like another. No new horrors, just old ones." She wondered if the letter would get by the censors.

Eugene was busy. Perhaps, to compensate for his unfair internment, someone was pulling strings. So many people were making so many unseen efforts. Sonya and Mrs. Levinger continued the quiet tasks of their Agency, more and more of them against the rules. The yellow-eyed man upstairs spent weeks at Bletchley Park. Lotte fiddled on corners when she had a free afternoon. Mr. Smith, so adept at inviting confidential disclosures, was discovered to be a spy, and was arrested.

Eugene wrote reviews for newspapers. Sonya helped

occasionally with sentence structure. New families wanted him to teach their children, practicing Czerny in formerly grand neighborhoods now sparkling with shards. He gave performances, too. He joined Lotte's quartet from time to time; and he played trios with Lotte and the cellist; and he played duets with Lotte. When the two could, they practiced in the church where Eugene and Sonya had listened to the Czech brother and sister. "Such a good piano," Eugene said.

Sonya brought her families to the concerts—the couple and their retarded daughter, once; the half-crazy mother and her little boys several times; the young waitresses; the pickpocket plasterers.

Of course—she told herself—all couples who played together developed affinities. Some had affinities from birth—consider those Czech twins, consider the Menuhins. Eugene and Lotte were not brother and sister, though they could be father and daughter. Twenty years lay between them. She calculated again. Twenty-four! She thought of the tenor... Eugene's brown profile bent over the keys. His mouth grimaced, sucked. Lotte nestled her chin onto her handkerchief. The fingers of her left hand danced. There were dark patches under the arms of the blue dress. At night, on her cot, she sometimes cried out, in French.

One evening Sonya came home to an empty room smelling of cigarettes. She put the milk she carried on the sill next to the geraniums. There was a chapel a block away—an ugly little dissenters' place. She sat in a back pew and rested her brow on the back of the pew in front of her, and lifted her head, and brought it down again on the wood, and lifted it, and brought it down.

III.

The first of the doodlebugs struck a week after the D-Day landings. They struck again and again. They were not like the bombs of the earlier Blitz. There was no time to get to a safe place; there was no safe place. People simply flattened themselves, waiting to be hurled, impaled, shattered, blown to bits, buried alive. If they were far enough away from the site they might be spared.

"The end is near, the end is near," the landlady told Sonya. "The end is near," sighed the parents of the damaged daughter. "Hitler's last gasp," declared Mrs. Levinger. Sonya thought that the Fuhrer seemed to have a lot of wind left in his lungs, but all she said was that the demented mother and her boys must be gotten out of London. "Maybe that house in Hull"; and for half an hour they discussed the pros and cons of the children being incarcerated in a virtual bedlam, each woman supplying the other's arguments like the friends they had become. They resolved on a more farm-like retreat, and Sonya made the arrangements.

Work continued, rebuilding continued; even concerts.

One day at half past noon Sonya was eating an apple on a bench in Hyde Park when she heard the familiar hum. She continued to chew. She saw the flying bomb, there was just one, it was only a bomb, they were all only bombs. Some, she'd been told, failed to explode. This one exploded, south of the Park. She was still chewing. Smoke rose, dark gray and thick, and the sounds she heard now were sirens, and further explosions and buildings crashing, and shrieks, and footsteps, her own among them, for she was running across the park, her apple still in her hand, toward the bomb, because the place of the bomb was the place of that church, wasn't it? And they were rehearsing this noontime, weren't they? She ran across the King's Road; and now she was part of a mob, some rushing along with her, some against her. Sides of houses had vanished. Faces were black. She stumbled over a woman, stopped; but the woman was dead. She ran on. An arm poked out of a heap of stones. She stopped again, and this time helped a fireman dig at the stones and extricate a woman, still alive thank God, and a baby protected by the woman's other arm, the baby too was alive thank God thank God. The smoke made it hard to breathe. Buildings kept falling. There was the smell of scorched flesh. Sonya reached the street of the church. The church was blasted. There was already a cordon; how fast the municipality had worked; no more than ten minutes had passed; these brave people; but she would simply have to get under the rope. Her apple was gone. She stooped. "Miss!" Somebody strong yanked her by her hips. She whirled into the arms of a red-faced man in a helmet; and saw, over his shoulder, Eugene, his brow dark, bruised in fact, and Lotte, filthy. They were holding hands. In her free hand Lotte held the instrument case. They had not been in the church, they explained when she reached them. They had lingered at home.

The barrage continued for months. Only storms kept the planes away. Sonya prayed for a hurricane. Churchill conceded that London was under attack. The flying bombs did not cease until three weeks before Victory.

But earlier still—five weeks before Victory—Lotte and Eugene left for Manchester. The director of the new civic orchestra there had heard Lotte playing with the quartet, had offered her a job. There would be pupils for Eugene.

Lotte had been sharing Eugene's bed since the day the doodlebug struck the church. But the night before leaving she scratched on Sonya's door. She put on the old clothes—the hat, the plaid trousers. She played "Some Day I'll Find You" and "I'll See You Again."

In the morning all three walked to the Tube and rode to the station. Even next to Eugene and Lotte, Sonya saw them as if from a distance—two gifted émigrés, ragged, paired. Father and daughter? Step-siblings? Nobody's business. As soon as they boarded the train they found a window and stared through it, their loved faces stony with love of her. She wondered how long Lotte would flourish under Eugene's brooding protection, how soon she would turn elsewhere. She was French, wasn't she, and Frenchwomen were faithless... His mother's diamond! She lifted her left hand in its disreputable glove and pointed toward the place of a ring with her right index finger.

On the other side of the window Eugene shook his head. *Yours,* he mouthed.

So Sonya sold the ring. It fetched less than she'd hoped—the stone was flawed. She bought a voluminous raincoat made out of parachute material. She bought new gloves and some dramatic trousers. She stashed the rest of the money.

IV.

"It's been a long time," said Sonya, when Mrs. Levinger had left them alone.

"Oh, I wanted to visit. When I was in Lisbon, in Amsterdam . . . But each time, something sent me elsewhere." He shifted in his ill-fitting jacket. He had lost more weight. Mrs. Levinger had hinted that he was some kind of hero.

They left the office and walked into wind and rain. Sonya's new coat swirled this way and that; it got drenched though it was supposed to be water repellent; it dragged her backwards. Finally she lifted its skirts, so as to be more easily blown to wherever he was taking her.

A pub. They sat down. Sonya knew he would not mention the nature of the work he had done; and he didn't—not during the first beer, not during the second. So: "Where now?" she asked, resting her worn-out hands on the worn-out table.

He told her about the Displaced Persons camps. He was going to the one at Oberammergau. "I hope you will join us. Your persistence, your intelligence, your accommodating nature . . ." She waved away his words with her right hand and he caught it midair. "I will stop this talk, though it is not flattery. I invite you to Oberammergau."

"I speak no German."

"But you are musical," he reminded her. He caught her other hand, though it couldn't be said to be in flight, was just lying there on the table. "Sonya Sofrankovitch. Will you come?"

She was silent for several minutes. His odd smile—would she ever get used to it, to him?—told her how much he wanted to hear Yes.

"Yes," she said.

Purim Night

Camp Gruenwasser was preparing for Purim, that merry celebration when you must drink until you cannot distinguish the king from the villain, the queen from the village tart.

"Purim?" Ludwig inquired.

He was twelve; pale and thin like all the others. But Ludwig had been pale and thin Before, during his pampered early boyhood in Hamburg. While hiding out with his uncle he had failed to become ruddy and fat.

"Purim is a holiday," Sonya said. She was fifty-six, also pale and thin by nature. She had spent the War in London; now she was co-director of this Camp for Displaced Persons, what a euphemism: fugitives from cruelty, they were; homeless, they were; despised. "Purim celebrates the release of the Jewish people. From a wicked man."

"Release. Released by the Allied Forces?"

"No, no. This was in Shushan, Shushan, Shushan, long ago . . ." She said 'long ago' in English. The rest of the conversation—all

183

their conversations in the makeshift, crowded office where Ludwig often spent the afternoon—was conducted in German. Ludwig's was the pedantic German of a precocious child, Sonya's the execrable German of an American with no talent for languages. Her Yiddish was improving at Camp Gruenwasser, though. Yiddish was the Camp's lingua franca, cigarettes its stable currency.

"Shushan, Shushan, Shushan," Ludwig repeated. "A place of three names?"

Sonya briefly closed her eyes. "I was repeating an old song, a line from an old song." She opened them again and met his reddish-brown gaze. "Haman was the name of the wicked man. The heroine was a queen, Esther. Speaking of queens . . ."

"We were not."

"We were not what?"

"We were not speaking of queens."

"Even so," said Sonya. "A set of chessmen came in with the allotments yesterday. It is lacking only a pawn. A stone—can you employ a stone?"

"Yes. Also my uncle keeps his corns in a box for just such purposes."

Sonya dragged a rickety chair to the wall underneath a shelf, and climbed up on it, and retrieved the box of chessmen. She gave it to Ludwig.

He was scurrying off when Ida said, "Wait." Ida was the secretary, a Person who had been a milliner Before. "I will tell about Purim, you should know, a Jewish boy like you."

He paused midflight, back against the wall, eyes wide as if under a searchlight. *"In Shushan, Shushan, Shushan* long ago," said Ida in English with a nod to Sonya; then continued in German, "there was

184

a King, Ahasuerus; and a General, Haman; and Mordecai, a wise Jew who spent his time by the gates of the Palace. King Ahasuerus's queen offended him so he called for a new Queen. Mordecai . . ." and she used an unfamiliar word.

Sonya ruffled through her German-English dictionary. "*Procured?* I'm not sure . . ."

". . . *procured* his niece, Esther," said Ida, her dark eyes insistent. "Mordecai refused to bow down to Haman. Haman arranged to murder the Jews. Esther, a Queen now, urged Ahasuerus to stop the murder. The Jews were saved."

"*Procured* . . ." Sonya still objected; and Ludwig, still pinned to the wall, said, "It was a miracle, then."

"A miracle," nodded Ida.

"I do not believe in miracles, especially miracles accomplished by the *fuck.*" The word wedged its Anglo-Saxon bluntness into the German polysyllables. The vocabulary of children had been augmented by American servicemen. But the GIs were not responsible for the hasty and brutal lovemaking Ludwig had witnessed in forest huts, in barns by the side of the road, in damp Marseilles basements.

"A girl with good looks and a beautiful hat can work miracles," Ida said. "Withholding the fuck. And that word, Ludwig, it is improper." She returned to her typewriter. Ludwig ran away.

Sonya, who had more to do today than three people could accomplish in a week, strolled to the narrow window. It was midafternoon. Shadows were deepening in the courtyard formed by the long wooden barracks so hastily abandoned by the Wehrmacht that Persons continued to find gun parts, buttons, medals, and fragments of letters (*"Heinz, leibling, der kinder . . ."*).

There was still a triangle of sunlight in the courtyard, though, and ragged children were playing within it, and Ludwig should be among them, would have been among them if he weren't a peculiar child who preferred the company of adults.

The year was 5707 by Biblical reckoning and 1947 by the Christian calendar. The Purim party would begin after dinner. There would be pastries—hamantaschen: Haman's hats. Without those pastries the holiday might as well be ignored; without those pastries the Megillah—the Tale, written on a scroll—might as well be stuffed into a cistern. Tonight's necessary hamantaschen—they would be a joke. Men who had been chefs Before knew how to bake sachartorte, linzertorte, all kinds of sweets; but where was the sugar, where the nuts? Today, using coarse flour and butter substitute and thin smears of blackberry preserves, they would bake ersatz hamantaschen, one or two per individual. Sonya did not know whether the practical bakers considered babies individuals, though babies certainly counted to the Red Cross and the American Command—each infant received its own vitamin-laced chocolate bars and its own Spam and its own cigarettes. Sonya could not procure sufficient tinned milk, however... As for the meal preceding the party; it would consist of the usual *drek:* watery spinach soup, potatoes, and black bread. Eisenhower had decreed that the Displaced Persons Camps be awarded 2000 calories per Person per day; decent of him; but the General couldn't keep count of newcomers, they came in so fast.

"In my atelier I served the most distinguished and cosmopolitan women," mused Ida, her hands at rest on the keyboard. "I fashioned turbans and cloches and toques."

"Cartwheels and mantillas," encouraged Sonya, who had heard this reminiscence before.

"I spoke five languages. I made..."

"Sonya!" came the voice of Roland, Roland Rosenberg, Sonya's co-director. "Sonya?" and he followed his voice into the office, his eyes flickering over the beauteous Ida and coming to rest on Sonya's narrow visage. He still had a fat man's grace, even a fat man's circumference, though he was losing weight like all the staff. "Sonya, the Chassids in the North Building refused to share their Megillah. They boycotted the general service."

"The Enlightenment Society also boycotted," Ida remarked. "They held a seminar on Spinoza."

"The blackberry jam—there's so little of it. Goddam!" said Sonya. She was subject to sudden ferocity these days. It was the Change, Ida told her knowingly, though Ida herself was only thirty-five.

"Poppy seeds—why couldn't they send poppy seeds, I requested poppy seeds," said Roland. Consulting a list, he left as unceremoniously as he had entered.

"Roland, it's all right," Sonya called after him. "The kindly German farmers—they will certainly butcher some calves for our party." She was in the doorway now, but he had rounded the corner. "Whipped cream will roll in like surf." She raised her voice, though he was surely out of earshot. "General Eisenhower—he will personally attend."

"Sonya," said Ida in a severe tone. "It is time for your walk."

About Purim Ludwig had dissembled. Feigning ignorance was always a good idea; know-it-alls, he'd observed, tended to get beaten up or otherwise punished. In fact, he'd already heard the Story of Esther, several times. First from the young man in the

Room next door, the one with the radiant face. Ludwig, recognizing the radiance, predicted that the young man would get caught in the next X-ray round-up. Meanwhile the feverish fellow did a lot of impromptu lecturing, even haranguing. Did he think he was the Messiah? grumbled Uncle Claud. One day last week he'd gathered a bunch of children around him and recited the Purim Tale. He made a good thing of it, Ludwig thought from the periphery of the circle; he almost foamed at the mouth when reciting the finale, the hanging of Haman and his ten sons, the slaughter of the three hundred conspirators. Then the Story had been taken up in the Schoolroom on the second floor of North Building, where grimy windows overlooked in succession the one-story kitchen; then the grubby garden, all root vegetables, well this was a stony patch, said Uncle Claud, his voice rumbling like a Baron's; we cannot expect the chanterelles we scraped from the rich soil in the South of France. Past the garden a road led between farms to the village of tiled roofs. Beyond the village green hills gently folded. The Judaica teacher, not looking through the window at this familiar view, had begun the Purim story by reading it in Hebrew, maybe half a dozen kids could understand. He translated into Yiddish and also Russian. His version, a droning bore in all three languages, insisted that the Lord, not Esther, had intervened to save the Jews. The History teacher said that night that there was no justification for this interpretation in Scripture. A day later the Philosophy Professor referred to the story as a metaphor.

"Metaphor?" inquired Ludwig; and presently learned the meaning of the term. He loved learning. He liked to hang around the office because Roland without making a big thing of it let fall so many bits of knowledge, farted them out like a horse. Sonya too was interesting to observe, hating to argue but having to argue, hating to persuade but having to persuade. She'd rather be by herself, reading or dreaming; Ludwig could tell; she reminded him of his mother... And Ida with her deep beautiful eyes and her passionate determination to go to Palestine; if only Uncle Claud would fuck her, maybe all three would end up in the Holy Land, well, not so Holy, but not a barracks either. He'd heard that people there lived in tents with camels dozing outside. But Uncle Claud preferred men.

Even without the Story Ludwig would have noticed Purim. The Persons in the Camp—those who were not disabled, paralyzed with despair, stuck in the TB hospital, too old, too young, or (by some mistake in assignment) Christian—the Persons were loudly occupied with the holiday. In the barrack Rooms, behind the tarps and curtain strips that separated cubicle from cubicle, costume makers rustled salvaged fabrics; in stairwells, humorists practiced skits; in the West Building raisins fermented and a still bubbled. In the village Persons were exchanging cigarettes and candy bars for the local wine. "Sour and thin," sneered Uncle Claud, who hid among his belongings a bottle of cognac procured God knew how. Uncle Claud smoked most of his cigarette allotment and also Ludwig's, and so he rarely had anything to barter. The cognac— Ludwig thought of it as a foretaste of the waters of Zion. "Zion has no waters," Uncle Claud insisted. Every night he gave Ludwig a fiery thimbleful, after their last game.

They owned a board. Sometimes they were able to borrow chessmen; but usually they used those of a Lithuanian in the next Room, the fervent Messiah's Room. The Lithuanian didn't care for chess but happened to own the set of his brother, now ashes. He wouldn't lend, wouldn't sell, would only lease. Claud had to relinquish a cigarette for the nightly pleasure. But now... Ludwig parted the shredded canvas that was their door, sat down on the lower bunk beside his uncle. "Look!" he said, and shook the box like a noisemaker.

Claud smiled and coughed. "The Litvak—he can kiss my backside."

When Sonya left the office, Ida resumed typing. She was doing requisitions: for sulpha drugs; for books; for thread; for food, food, food.

> Dear Colonel Spaulding,
> You are correct that the 2000 calories Per Person Per Day are Supplemented by Red Cross packages and purchases from the village. But the Red Cross packages come unpredictably. Some of our Persons will not eat Spam. And though we must turn a blind eye to the Black Market, it seems unwise to encourage its use. Our severest need now is dried fruit—our store of raisins is completely wiped out—and sanitary napkins.
>
> Yours Very Truly,
> Sonya Sofrankovich

Ida ran a hand through her hair. Her hair was as dense and dark as it had been ten years earlier, when she had been captured, separated from the husband now known to be dead, oh Shmuel, and forced to work in a Munitions Factory. Not labor camp, not escape from labor camp, not the death in her arms of her best friend, oh Luba, not recapture, not liberation; not going unwashed for weeks, not living on berries in the woods, not the disappearance of her menses for almost a year and their violent return; not

190

influenza lice odors suppurations; not the discovery in the forest of an infant's remains, a baby buried shallowly, dug up by animals; not the one rape and the many beatings—nothing had conquered the springiness of her hair. Her hair betrayed her expectance of happiness. And where would she find this happiness? Ah, *b'eretz:* in the Land. Milliners, she had been informed by the Emissary from the Underground, barely concealing his disgust… Milliners were not precisely what the Land required. Do you think we wear chapeaux while feeding our chickens, Giverit? Perhaps you intend to drape our cows with silken garlands. Sitting on a wooden chair, hands folded in her lap, she told him that she would change careers with readiness, transform herself into a milkmaid, till the fields, draw water, shoot Arabs, blow up Englishmen. Then she leaned toward this lout of a pioneer. "But if cities arise *b'eretz*, and commerce, and romance—I'll make hats again." He looked at her for a long time. Then he wrote her name on his list. Now she was waiting for the summons.

Meanwhile she typed applications for other Persons. Belgium had recently announced that it would take some. Australia also. Canada too. America was still dithering about its immigration laws, although the Lutheran Council of the American Midwest had volunteered to relocate fifty Persons, not specifying agricultural workers, not even specifying Lutherans. But how many tailors could this place Minnesota absorb?

She typed an application, translating from the Yiddish handwriting. *Name: Morris Losowitz;* yes, she knew him as Mendel but Morris was the proper Anglicization. *Age: 35;* yes that was true. *Dependents: Wife and three Children;* yes that was true too, though it ignored the infant on the way. *Occupation: Electrical Engineer.*

In Poland he had taught in a Cheder. Perhaps he knew how to change a light bulb. *Languages Spoken in order of Fluency: Yiddish, Polish, Hebrew, English.* Strictly true. He could say I Want To Go To America, and maybe a dozen other words. His wife spoke better English, was more intelligent; but the Application wasn't curious about her.

Ida typed on and on. The afternoon darkened further. Her own overhead light bulb shook on its noose. In the Big Hall above her ceiling raged a joyous battle: walls were being decorated, the camp's orchestra was practicing, the Purimspielers were perfecting their skits.

She stopped, and covered her typewriter with the remnants of a tallis. She locked the office and went into the courtyard. Two members of the DP police stood there, self-important noodles. They grinned at her. She passed children still playing in the chill dark. She entered the East Building. What a din: groups of men, endlessly arguing. And those two Hungarian sisters, always together, their hands clasped or at least their knuckles touching. She'd heard that they accompanied each other into the toilet. In the first Room there was a vent to the outdoors and somebody had installed a stove, and always a cabbage stew boiled, or a pot of onions, and always washed diapers hung near the steam, never getting entirely dry. Hers was the next Room, hers the first cubicle, a nice old lady slept in the bed above, preferring elevation to the rats she believed infested the place, though there had been no rats since the visit of a Sanitary Squad from the British Zone. But the lady expected their return, and never left her straw mattress until midafternoon.

She was up and about now, gossiping somewhere. From beneath the bed Ida dragged a sack and dumped its contents onto her own mattress—a silk blouse, silk underwear, sewing utensils, glue, and a Wehrmacht helmet, battered and cracked. And Cellophane; Cellophane wrappers; dozens of Cellophane wrappers, hundreds of Cellophane wrappers; some crushed, some merely torn, some intact, slipped whole from the Lucky Strikes and Camels that they had once protected . . . She began to work.

Sonya, ejected from her office by the solicitous Ida, had only pretended to be taking a walk. When out of the range of the office window she doubled back to the South Building. Two women in South were near their time, though neither was ready to be transported to the Lying-In Bungalow. In their Room they were being entertained by three men rehearsing a Purimspiel: a Mordecai with a fat book, an Ahasuerus in a cloak, and a Fool, in a cap with a single bell. A Fool? The Purimspiel had a long connection to the *commedia dell'arte*, Roland had mentioned. This Fool played a harmonica, the King sang *Yedeh hartz hot soides*— Every heart has secrets—and Mordecai, his book open, rocked from side to side and uttered wise sayings.

Sonya next went to the storehouse. Someone had stolen a carton of leftover Hanukah supplies donated by a congregation in New Jersey. Not a useful donation—the Camp would be disbanded by next December, every resident knew that for a fact, all of them would be housed comfortably in Sydney, Toronto, New York, Tel Aviv. . . Still, shouted the Person in charge, this is a crazy insult, stealing from ourselves; why don't we rob the swine in the village?

The TB hospital next, formerly the Wehrmacht's stable. The Military Nurse who ran the place snapped that all was as usual, two admissions yesterday, no discharges, X-ray machine on its last legs, what else was new. Her assistants, female Persons who had been doctors Before, were more informative. "Ach, the people here now will sooner or later get better probably," one said. "They'll recover, nu, if God is willing, maybe if He isn't, if He just looks the other way. Choose Life. Isn't it written?"

Sonya went to her own bedroom. As Camp Directors she and Roland occupied private quarters—a single narrow room with a triple-decker bed. Roland slept on the bottom, Sonya in the middle, once in a while an inspector from Headquarters occupied the top, where else to put him? There was a sink and a two-drawer dresser. Sonya opened the lower drawer and reached into the back. Why should she too not dress up for the Purim Party? Choose Life, Choose Beauty, Choose what all American women long for, a little black dress. She grabbed the rolled-up garment she had stashed there two years ago and brought it into the weak light and raised it and shook it. It unfurled reluctantly. She took off her shirt, slipped the dress over her head, stepped out of her ski pants. The dress felt too large. There was a piece of mirror resting slantwise on the sink—Roland used it for shaving. She straightened it. Then she backed away.

A witch peered at her from the jagged looking glass. A skinny powerless witch with untamed gray hair wearing the costume of a bigger witch.

She had been a free spirit once, she thought she recalled. At the young age of fifty she had dwelled on a Rhode Island beach; she had danced under the moon. She had known the Hurricane. She had lived in a bed-sitter in London and had worked for the Joint Distribution Committee. She had saved some children. She had known the doodlebugs. In a damp pub in 1945 she had accepted Roland Rosenberg's invitation to run Camp Gruenwasser with him. She had allowed his fat, freckled hand to rest on hers.

She peered closer at the tiny witch in the glass. And then some disturbance in the currents of the air caused the mirror to hurl itself onto the wooden floor. There it splintered.

Roland would have to shave without a mirror. Maybe he'd grow a beard.

She was attempting to pick up the shards when he came in.

"Sonya, stop." He walked down the hall and fetched the communal broom and dustpan—a large thistle on a stick, a piece of tin. She was sucking her finger when he returned. He looked at the cut. "Run it under water for a long time." She ran it under water for a long time. When she turned around the damage was swept up, the implements had been returned, and he was lying on the lowest bed, eyes closed, as if it was this recent effort that had exhausted him, not two years of constant toil.

She closed their door. She unbuckled his worn belt. She unbuttoned his flannel shirt. What color had it been originally? It had long ago faded to the yellowish gruenwasser of his eyes. She unbuttoned the cuffs too, but did not attempt to remove the shirt—it was up to him whether or not to take it off; he was a sentient being, wasn't he? Was he? He had all the vitality of a corpse. But when she roughly rolled down his trousers and pulled *them* off and rolled down his undershorts and pulled them off, she saw that he was ready for her. When had they done this last—three months ago? Six? For them, as for the Persons, one gray day got sucked into the next. Yet there were joys: letters from relatives thought dead; meat sometimes in the soup; and tonight, a party...
She stood and lifted her little black dress over her witch's body. It

195

ruffled her witch's coiffure. She left the dress lying on the floor. She straddled Roland's erection, brushing him back and forth, side to side, until she felt a spurt of her own moisture, and he must have felt it too, for, alert, he gripped her upper arms and turned them both over at once as if they were a single animal, a whale in green flannel maybe. She looked up at him. "Roland, I love you," she said, for the first time ever. And she did, she loved the whole silly mess of him: the effeminate softness of his shoulders, the loose flesh under his chin, the little eyes, the breath redolent of processed meats, the sparse eyebrows, the pudgy hands, the fondness for facts. Were these not things to love? Oh, and the kindness. He thrust, thrust, Ah, she said; and even in her pleasure, her witch's pleasure, she heard the stealthy opening of the door. She turned her head and met Ludwig's rodent gaze.

By the time Roland and Sonya arrived at the Great Hall—a big room with a little stage—the thrown-together orchestra was playing: strings, one trumpet, woodwinds; an accordion, a balalaika; three guitars, one drum. Candles in tin cans were burning side by side on the rim of the stage, and on a ledge around the room, and at the windows. Each thick candle, Sonya noticed, was made up of a clutch of little, twisted candles, the Hanukah kind. There were also several Hanukiahs. A broad table held a mountain of hamantaschen. Another table sagged under bowls of liquid. "Let's hope no one got hold of the methanol," said Roland. At another Camp, mostly Polish Persons, two men had gone blind from drinking the stuff.

Roland was dressed, he claimed, as Dionysius—that is, two sprigs of juniper were pinned to his scant hair, one falling onto his forehead, the other nestling within his humble nape.

Most costumes were equally rudimentary. Where could Persons get fabric, jewels, gauzy shawls? Yet some had indeed procured such items. A wife had made a royal garment for her husband. It was a short black silk cape, formerly the lining of their only coat. They wouldn't need a lined coat in Palestine, this loving spouse explained to Sonya. She had adorned the cape with little white fur tails which on close inspection turned out to be the inner stuff of sanitary napkins. Several young Mordecais wore, in front of their ears, scholarly coils: the strapping tape from Red Cross packages. One Esther had saved a beaded dress from her dead mother's wardrobe. Another wore a dirndle skirt and a jersey shirt that said *Englewood High School.* A Catholic family slipped in shyly wearing Easter finery; after years in a cardboard valise the clothing too seemed to be cardboard. Ludwig and his Uncle Claud had encased their upper bodies in splintery barrels that had held potatoes. Their heads were crowned by circlets of dry leaves. *Schwarz Konig* was painted on Ludwig's barrel. Uncle Claud was the White Queen.

King, Queen, Wise Man, and the occasional hero: cigar stubs identified Churchill, a cigarette holder Roosevelt. No one came dressed as Haman. Haman adorned the yellow walls, though. He was painted in green, painted in black tar, drawn in pencil, cut from brown paper. There were several Hamans in relief, made from a sturdy papier-mâché. "What is this stuff?" Sonya asked the History teacher. "The *Stars and Stripes,* pulped," he told her. Many Hamans were rendered feet up, head down. Every one wore a little black mustache.

The orchestra fluted, blared, strummed. Persons danced, changed partners, danced again. The pile of hamantaschen

197

diminished, was replenished. The two Hungarian sisters entered, hand in hand. A skit was performed in one corner. Ida entered, wearing a hat. A skit was performed on the stage. Someone sang, dreadfully. Three men dragged in the upright piano from the corridor, although the orchestra had specified that it did not require a piano, did not want a piano, certainly could not employ that piano, which was missing seventeen keys. The orchestra leader swiped at one of the three moving men with his baton, an umbrella spoke. Roland intervened. The piano, with bench but without pianist, remained, near the string section. The radiant young man from the South Building entered, wrapped in a blue-and-white tablecloth with permanent stains; Sonya guessed that it too came from Englewood, New Jersey. The philosophy teacher...

Was that woman Ida? Sonya had never before seen her in lipstick; she must have been hoarding it forever; lucky it hadn't pulverized. And that brilliant red silk blouse, how come *it* wasn't dust... Ida blew a kiss to Sonya. Ida asked Mendel to dance. Mendel's wife, vastly pregnant, smiled acquiescence. Mendel was dressed in a long black jacket whose wide belt bore a buckle covered in silver foil. Sonya guessed his Puritan garb was intended as Lutheran. Ida danced with others. Her hat glistened in one part of the room, glowed in another. It was a heavy cloche with a narrow brim, and it was covered with hundreds of shining bows, or perhaps butterflies, or perhaps ecstatic transparent birds. They caught the light of the candles, transforming that light into ruby twinkles, turquoise wings, flashes of green. Were they silk, those bows butterflies birds? Were they diamonds? Were they real winged creatures? Ida whirled by. Below the iridescent helmet her hair thickly curled; some curls, damp and enticing, clung to her neck. "We have guests," Roland said in Sonya's ear.

She had been ignoring the three American officers, though she had identified their rank, she had noticed their medals, she had recognized the famous grin. "Roland I am exhausted, my charm whatever there was of it is used up, would you take care of them for a while Roland? And tell them that your wife will be with them shortly."

"Wife?"

"Everybody thinks we're married, why upset that cart..."

"I wish you were my wife. I would like you to be my wife."

"Yes," she said, acknowledging his wish, maybe even acceding to it; and then she backed up, backed up, until she collided with the accordionist moving forward. The Persons' orchestra was taking a break. Sonya sat down at the ruined piano.

She played "You and the Night and the Music." The missing keys were mostly at either end; the absence of middle A and the B-flat below middle C was a nuisance, but she fudged. She played a Strauss waltz and the waltz from Faust. The smoke thickened like roux. The air in the room was clouded and warm and vital; life itself might have originated in these emanations from burning tobacco. She played "Smoke Gets in Your Eyes." She played "The Merry Widow."

The noise increased. There was some yelling: another skit. She saw Ida waltzing with the General. Ida looked up at him from under her hat. As they turned Sonya saw an inquiring look on her lovely face. As they turned again she saw the look turn into one of admiration. As they turned again she saw the look become one of pleasure.

"She's fucking him," said Ludwig, in English. He had taken off his Black King's barrel; he was seated on the bench beside her; he smelled of brandy. "I am employing a metaphor," he explained.

The General danced a two-step with Ida's cubicle-mate, the little old lady who came alive at dusk. He danced the Kazachok with a group of Ukrainians. He danced another waltz with Ida. And then, twenty minutes later, Sonya and Roland and Ludwig and Ida and a dozen others stood at the gates to wave good-bye to the jeep carrying the three officers. The General touched his cap—handsome headgear, really, with all that gold insignia, but no match for Ida's.

Sonya predicted that the Camp's rations would soon increase, but they did not. She hoped that Ida might get a private gift—silk stockings, maybe—but nothing appeared. She even thought that the new immigration act would be rushed through the United States Congress.

"It was only a dance," shrugged Ida.

"Two dances. And you were ravishing."

"He's a soldier," Ida sighed. "Not a king."

But then something did happen. The allotment of cigarettes per Person was officially increased, but the augmented allotment was not to be distributed (a formal letter ordered) but to remain in the disposition of the Directors. And that, Sonya and the newly bearded Roland discovered, was enough to change things significantly—to get butter, milk, greens, sanitary napkins; to buy a sow, which enraged some but fed others; to pay a glazier from the village to fix broken windows; to procure gas for mendicant trips to Frankfurt which resulted in more butter, milk, greens, and sanitary napkins; and finally, with the aid of a bundle of additional dollars contributed by Americans, to enable a sizeable group of Persons to bribe its way overland to Brindisi where waited a boat bound for Haifa.

Purim Night

One day Mendel's wife, who had replaced Ida as the Directors' secretary, handed Sonya a letter.

"We have reached Palestine," wrote Ludwig, in Hebrew. "We have been saved, again."

The
Coat

"Other capitals," began Roland, and paused for breath as he sometimes did. Sonya waited with apparent serenity. "...are in worse shape," he concluded.

They were standing on the Pont Neuf, holding hands. All at once they embraced, as if ravaged Paris demanded it.

Roland Rosenberg was sixty and Sonya Rosenberg was fifty-eight. They had directed Camp Gruenwasser since 1945; but finally the place had been able to close, its last Displaced Persons repatriated to Romania. So the Rosenbergs too had left, traveling westwards on first one train and then another. Each was dressed in prewar clothing, each lugged a single misshapen suitcase. They looked like Displaced Persons themselves; but their American passports gave them freedom, and their employment by the Joint Distribution Committee gave them cash.

Paris was giving them dusty cafés, a few concerts with second-rate performers, black bread, and this old bridge called New.

203

Recovering from their embrace, they turned again toward the river. "The Old World," said Roland, "is a corpse."

Sonya—who had spent the war years in blistered London and the five decades previous in Rhode Island—knew The Old World only by reputation. Cafés, galleries, libraries, chamber recitals; salons de thé; polyglots in elegant clothing conducting afternoon dalliances before returning to one of the great banking houses . . . A derelict barge sailed toward them, sailed under them: thin children without shoes played on its deck.

On their third day, coming out of a brasserie near the Bastille, Roland suffered a heart attack. He spent a week in the hospital. Sonya sat by his side in a long room with metal cots and wooden floors that, like Camp Gruenwasser's infirmary, stank of carbolic acid. She displayed an outward calm, she even felt calm—he would survive this attack, the French doctors told her, with emphasis on the *this*—but she could not prevent her long fingers from raking her long hair, hair that had turned from gray to white during the War and its aftermath.

When Roland was released they traveled by train to Le Havre and by ship to New York. The Joint got them a place on Lower Fifth.

It was a meandering apartment with mahogany furniture and gilded mirrors and draperies in a deep red. Circus wagon, Sonya might have called that shade, but she knew that colors had acquired new names since her departure in 1940, almost a decade ago—names borrowed from wines and liqueurs: cassis, port, champagne, chartreuse. The apartment was rent-free—that is, the Joint paid its rent to the regular tenant, who was away in California for a year. At the end of the year Roland and Sonya would find something more to their mutual taste, whatever that turned out to be. At Camp Gruenwasser they had shared an office and then a bedroom; they had married six months ago; but they had not yet together made a home.

Right away Sonya got her hair cut. The actress Mary Martin was playing a Navy nurse in a Broadway show. Mary Martin's hair was clipped close to the scalp, like a boy's. All over Manhattan women were trying that coiffure, most of them just once—even the prettiest face looked plain without surrounding fluff. But the cropped style suited Sonya's long head and steady eyes. "You're always beautiful to me," said Roland when she came nervously home from the beauty shop. The effect of his declaration was stronger because of the flatness of its tone. "I'll love you until the day I die," he added, again without emotion; and she knew that to be true too. Let the day be slow in coming, she thought, again smelling the carbolic of the hospital.

Roland's skin was still pasty but he was less often short of breath—a new medicine was helping. The Joint kept asking him to make speeches; well, of course, who knew more about the plight of European Jews during the previous two decades; who could judge better the situation of those who were left on the continent; who could better suppose the future. He came home from speech-giving with his shirt moist. Thank God the apartment building had an elevator.

The apartment's permanent tenant was a woman, they thought—they judged partly from the four-poster's silk spread, creamy yellow. Eggnog? There was a crumpled lace-trimmed handkerchief in the back of one of the dresser drawers; it smelled of perfume. The tenant read German; German books were everywhere. "She *is* German," concluded Sonya.

"Or Austrian or Swiss," said Roland. "Or Lithuanian."

"She's no Litvak," Sonya insisted, helplessly remembering Baltic Persons shivering in Gruenwasser's underheated barracks. "She's an aristocrat."

"There are Lithuanian aristocrats," began the reasonable man; but Sonya was already enumerating the signs of *hoch* culture: millefleur paperweights; framed eighteenth-century drawings; volumes of Rilke and Novalis; a shelf of novels in French. And the family photographs on the desk: a bespectacled father, a fine-featured mother—how would *she* fare with a Mary Martin chop?—five blonde daughters in the loose children's dresses of the twenties. The photographs seemed unposed—perhaps a favorite uncle had taken them, Roland suggested. The girls, very young, played in a garden; mountains rose in the distance. Slightly older, they occupied a living room—three lolled on a couch, another sat at a piano, the littlest looked out the window. At the foot of a gangplank the entire family stood close together, as if bundled. They were all in coats except for the father, who carried his over his arm. Mama wore an asymmetrical hat. The girls—teenagers now—wore cloches.

"They got out in time," said Roland.

"They're not Jewish. Intellectuals, though, liberals..."

"National Socialism had no use for them. Which one is our landlady, do you think?"

Sonya peered at the faces, alike but different—one wore glasses, one had very full lips... Roland coughed, touched his chest. "The curly one," Sonya decided.

And so, the identity of their more-or-less landlady more-or-less established, they turned to other things. Roland's job at the Joint kept him busy, and Sonya was playing hausfrau and taking long walks. She got to know the butcher, the grocer, the fishmonger. She was a steady customer at the hardware shop and the lending library and the dry cleaning establishment. She patronized a coffee shop on Fourth Avenue, and established an ersatz friendship with its proprietress. Through the Joint she and Roland met apprehensive immigrants and were kind to them. And Sonya made two real friends: women who'd known one of her cousins—a jewelry designer on the East Side, a social worker on the West. Sometimes, on weekends, Sonya and Roland went to the movies with these women and their husbands, or out to a restaurant. *Normal life,* she exulted. She thought of Ida, the Camp secretary, maybe safe in Israel née Palestine, maybe killed by mortar fire.

There was an armoire in the room they called the study. Sonya had stored her few summer dresses in the right side of it, and Roland's one summer suit. He had a winter suit, too. Insufficient; the Joint asked him to provide himself with a tuxedo at its expense. He was more and more in demand as a speaker, requested now by organizations of wealthy philanthropists, not just Zionists and Socialists. Roland reluctantly bought a tuxedo at Macy's and Macy's altered it to fit. It was delivered on a Saturday.

"I'll hide it in that armoire," he said. "And I'll hope that I don't ever have to pull it out, that those fellows find somebody else to harangue them. Just thinking of their dinners I get heartburn," and he groaned in his easy chair.

"Don't get up; I'll put it away," said Sonya quickly.

She opened the left door of the armoire; and held the tuxedo high, like a lamp. It was shrouded in the new element plastic. She

207

attempted to hang it, and encountered resistance. Something was already hanging there. She opened the right door and thrust the tuxedo among the summer clothes. Then she took down the something.

It was a long black narrow coat of soft wool. It was double-breasted: buttons on its right side, buttonholes on its left, and so—she had to look down at her own striped cotton blouse to be sure—it was a coat designed for a man. It had a shawl collar of fur—brown fur, mink probably. Her friend the jewelry designer had a mink jacket, its glossy hairs similar to this. There was a producer who lived on West End Avenue; Sonya had seen him in his famous mink greatcoat.

She peeked into the living room. Roland was dozing now, the newspaper in disarray across his lap. She took the coat from the wooden hanger and, carrying it across her two extended arms, brought it into the bedroom.

There she put it on. The stripes of her blouse peeped between the crescents of fur like some other species. This coat needed a brandy-colored silk scarf costing perhaps one month of Roland's salary, perhaps two. A bit of black would suffice. She reached into her middle drawer, pulled out a black slip, draped it within the collar. There.

Women's slacks were just catching on. They were not generally for street wear, unless the streets were in the Village. Sonya had adopted them enthusiastically. They suited her long stride. She could buy men's pants off the rack. She was wearing black trousers today, and oxfords.

A pier glass stood between the two bedroom windows. She walked slowly toward it.

What a distinguished gentleman. How well the white-haired

The Coat

head sat above the fur collar. The owner of this coat must be a slender fellow—the garment barely skimmed Sonya's thin frame. A man like this had had the cash to get out of Vienna, then get out of Paris, then get to New York—not like the little shoemaker Yenkel and his numerous children, not like chess-playing Claud, smoking and coughing on his lower bunk...

She took off the coat and brought it into the living room. Roland was awake. She showed him the garment like a saleslady, displaying the fine workmanship of the buttoned right cuff. The other cuff, she discovered, had lost its button.

"Very nice, but no use in California," said Roland. "So she left it in New York."

"He."

"He, I suppose. We might have figured. A woman irons." There'd been no ironing board when they arrived; they'd had to buy one. "A woman would have chosen different draperies—a softer color. Yes: this is a man's apartment."

"There's no spice rack above the stove," Sonya said. Roland gave her a thoughtful look. She turned from him and laid the coat at an angle on the Biedermeier sofa, its shoulders against the strict back, its skirts spread on the seat.

"But the photographs," Roland said suddenly.

"Oh, your first guess must have been right." She turned from the coat and walked back to Roland. "The pictures of that pretty family were taken by the coat's owner, our landlord, the beloved young uncle."

"No longer young," he sighed.

"Still beloved," and she touched his arm.

She took the coat to the neighborhood yarn shop—its missing button preyed on her conscience like a hungry pet. "Can you match this?" Sonya handed the buttoned right sleeve to the woman on the other side of the counter. The rest of the coat remained in her protective embrace.

"Ach, you don't meet such buttons any more. May I see the others?" Without waiting for permission the woman leaned forward and grasped the coat under the arms and took it from Sonya and laid it on the counter. She examined the carved leather hemispheres on the breast. She raised little green eyes to Sonya's. "We have nothing like this here. I would not know where to look, though in Budapest . . ." and she trailed off sentimentally. "But maybe!" She thrust her ringed hand into the coat's pocket, a pocket that Sonya had not guessed was there, so flat it was, so cleverly disguised by the seam. "Ach," she said again. "He knew it was loose, ripped it off, kept it safe."

"Who?"

"Your employer." Sonya had pulled on an old cardigan sweater against the October chill. She supposed she did look like a housekeeper. "A tailor should sew this on; don't try it yourself."

The tailor on University Place did the job while she waited. A sudden wind swept newspapers against the shop's grimy window. Once outside Sonya noticed that the temperature had dropped. So she put on the coat.

Only three blocks to home—one westwards, two north. She was moving like a chess knight. No, a king. No, no, how self-important—minor nobility.

Roland wasn't yet home. So she let the coat sit in his chair until,

The Coat

after five, the elevator began swishing up and down. Then she stowed it.

The next afternoon it kept her company in the kitchen while she cooked.

Another afternoon, while she lay on the bed reading, the coat slumped on a rosé chaise.

She did not wear it again until after the Christmas holidays. Then there was a cold snap. Her own coat was warm, yes; but would not the old gentleman's be warmer still?—its lining, unseen between silk and wool, was light yet effective. When she held the fabric between thumb and fingers something slid within, as if alive.

She bought it a scarf—not real silk, something synthetic, oh, these new fabrics. The color was perfect—cognac. She bought cashmere-lined leather gloves on sale. In a thrift shop she found a hat in the shape of a squat cylinder, mink-dyed squirrel.

Her daily walks became longer. She began on Fifth, turned onto Broadway at Union Square, stayed on its sunny side. In half an hour she was among the émigrés. She would not enter the cafeterias, where forgotten journalists argued all afternoon. But there was a café run by a sly man with a twirled mustache, and that place she did patronize. He was Bulgarian, she thought—her work at Camp Gruenwasser had made her adept at guessing nationalities. At the Bulgarian's were newspapers, chess games, waiters in discolored white jackets. Soon Sonya had her own table by the window, and she could order her omelet by raising an index finger. The coat lay on its side across the other chair. Hat and gloves and scarf nestled under the sleeping arm. Keys and wallet reposed in her trousers.

She went to art gallery openings. The openings were free, as was the champagne and canapés. She went to noontime concerts in churches, also free, though lacking refreshments. Warmly she stood in the unimproved area behind the Library, and fed pigeons. She went to a Saturday morning service at a Reform Temple—Roland always slept late on weekends. She went to a big Conservative Synagogue. She went to an old shul, and sat downstairs.

She did not think of the coat as lawfully hers, oh, no. But in its illicit protection she became a personage. Immigrant men hoping to adapt to the New World were buying fedoras and secondhand broad-shouldered suits. Unwittingly they looked like gangsters. In print dresses their wives resembled charladies. Sonya, American by birth, graduate of a teacher's college and an accounting course, never out of the country until she was past fifty… Sonya was preserving the Old World of ringstrasses, universities, coffeehouses, salons, museums, bunds and diets and Parliaments and banks. She walked and walked. Truck drivers shouted coarse phrases to one another. Shopgirls out for lunch wore glistening lipstick. Sometimes she paused at a department store window and bowed at her reflection.

One March Wednesday she went to a student recital at a private school. It was an Episcopalian establishment, but some German-Jewish families had been sending children there for a few generations. The school occupied a block of brownstones whose shared walls had been removed, so that behind the burghers' façade was a surprising interior: hallways hung with kindergarten art, an aquarium, the buzz of hopeful activity. A little auditorium was embedded within the whole. Sonya found a seat in the middle of a middle row. She saw from the program that she was to be treated to recitations, musical performances, a ballet…

The Coat

"Your grandchild is performing?" said the person next to her: a hammered pageboy under a beret, a badly reconstructed nose.

"Yes . . . she will dance."

"Ah," slightly friendly. "What is her name?" slightly interested.

"She is my daughter's child," said the barren Sonya. "*My* name is . . ."

The headmaster mounted the stairs to the stage, and Sonya's neighbor turned her worshipful gaze toward him, so Sonya had to be content with the botched rhinoplasty of the profile.

". . . Gruenwasser," she finished.

But the woman was no longer listening. Who wanted to listen to a refugee from God knows where. Delicate voices on the stage were singing Stephen Foster. The children's chorus at the Camp had managed Berlioz; well, they'd been directed by a once notable baritone from Dresden. He was in Argentina now. She wondered how he was faring among the gauchos.

The recital ended. Half an hour later, stepping out of the elevator, Sonya heard the telephone ringing in the apartment.

"Mrs. Rosenberg? This is Dr. Katz at the Montefiore hospital . . ." She threw keys and wallet onto the telephone table. ". . . has sustained a heart attack, he's very much alive . . ." She unbuttoned the coat and allowed it to drop to the floor. ". . . and conscious. His condition is stable . . ." She stepped away from the fallen coat, kicked it, got the room number, hung up, grabbed her raincoat from the closet—really, spring had come at last—and retrieved wallet and keys from the table. She snatched up the square of challis Roland had given her for her birthday—paisley, it was all the rage. She ran down the five flights of stairs and hailed a taxi. In the cab she tied the paisley under her chin.

213

"Thank you for coming."

"Thank you for inviting us." Where should they sit, Sonya
wondered. She watched Roland settle himself in his customary
chair, and so she took her own. Their hostess sat at ease on the sofa.

She was not the curly daughter, she was the one with full lips.
The lips were still full—she could not be more than thirty-five,
after all—and the long hair was still blonde. On the telephone: "I
want to meet you," she said in a husky voice that she must have
been told many times was irresistible; well, maybe it was
irresistible; *they* hadn't resisted. "You left me a nicer apartment
than the one I left you," she'd gone on. "Nothing out of place; and
those improvements!" The spice rack, Sonya supposed; the ironing
board, a chair leg that no longer wobbled, added plants...the
button? "Besides," she'd chuckled. "You forgot your tuxedo."

Now Madame Schumacher—"Can't I be Erika?"—poured
generous tots of sherry. "You're living on the West Side?"

In their building the elevator always clanged. They had no
second bedroom. On Roland's bad nights he sat up reading and
Sonya slept on the living room couch. There she dreamed of
London and the bombs. But the place caught afternoon sun. They
had purchased cotton rugs and secondhand furniture. Then they
had splurged on a Finnish chest painted with stylized flowers. They
used it as a coffee table.

"The West Side, yes," said Sonya.

"An easy bus ride to Carnegie Hall," said Roland; and so they
talked of music, and of the Mayor, and of films.

"Were you in Hollywood?" Sonya asked. Direct questions were
not her habit; but she was a quarter-century older than this

beautiful woman; and her navy shirtwaist gave her the modest authority of a nanny. She had abandoned the Mary Martin hairstyle; her straight white hair just grazed the shirtwaist's collar.

"The whole family is in the movie business, none of us in front of the camera. I did some translations, this and that... I was divorcing when I left New York and I am thoroughly divorced now." She gave a graceful shudder. Her accent was light, not at all guttural, just a sometime transposition of Ws and Vs, as in 'diworced.' The sisters had all learned English from their tutor, she said; and she, Erika, had worked on French during a summer spent with an aunt, such a beautiful apartment, you could see the Seine. Sonya thought of the ailing Paris, the oily river, the bridge.

More conversation, then silence. They would not see each other again: the woman-of-the world, the pair of pensioners. When Sonya and Roland got up to say good-bye, Erika stood also and left the room and came back with the tuxedo over her arm. "I didn't notice it when I first came home; it was hiding behind Franz's old coat."

"Oh Yes The Coat," said Sonya.

"My ex-husband's. I kept it out of malice, he loved it so. I think I'll give it to the Writers and Artists Thrift Shop."

"Our organization distributes clothing to the needy."

"I'll remember that," said Erika. She'd forget it before the elevator reached the lobby.

On the sidewalk, Roland pointed to the tuxedo, which Sonya carried over her arm. "I'll never wear that thing again."

"Who knows? 'With proper care you can live another twenty years,'" quoting his doctor.

"Proper care does not include after-dinner speeches in a monkey suit."

"Yes, well." And the coat, the coat . . .

"The tuxedo . . . will do for a shroud."

. . . the coat: she would haunt the Writers and Artists Thrift Shop until the thing appeared. She'd buy it and stash it in the Finnish chest; maybe in that relic the Old World would find repose. And if not, let it writhe. Love, love . . . "A shroud? Up yours," snorted Sonya, startling him, making him smile. "I intend to keep you around. Darling, let's have dinner out."

She took his arm and led him to a new Italian place on East Twelfth, one which the courtly old gentleman in the fur-collared coat had never had a chance to patronize.

The Story

"Predictable," said Judith da Costa.

"Oh...hopeful," said her husband Justin in his determinedly tolerant way.

"Neither," said Harry Savitsky, not looking for trouble exactly; looking for engagement perhaps; really looking for the door, but the evening had just begun.

Harry's wife Lucienne—uncharacteristically—said nothing. She was listening to the tune: a mournful bit from Smetana.

What these four diners were evaluating was a violinist, partly his performance, partly his presence. The new restaurant—Harry and Lucienne had suggested it—called itself The Hussar, and presented piroshki and goulash in a gypsy atmosphere. The chef was rumored to be twenty-six years old. The Hussar was taking a big chance on the chef, on the fiddler, on the location, and apparently on the help; one busboy had already dropped a pitcher of water.

"It's tense here, in the dining room," Judith remarked.

"In the kitchen—don't ask," said Harry.

In some accommodating neighborhood in Paris, a restaurant like The Hussar might catch on. In Paris...but this was not Paris. It was Godolphin, a town that was really a western wedge of Boston; Godolphin, home to Harry and Lucienne Savitsky, retired high-school teachers; Godolphin, not so much out of fashion as beyond its reach.

One might say the same of Harry. His preferred haberdashery was the Army/Navy surplus store downtown. Lucienne, however, was genuinely Parisian (she had spent the first four years of her life there, never mind that the city was Occupied, never mind that she was hardly ever taken out of the apartment) and she had a Frenchwoman's flair for color and line. As a schoolgirl in Buenos Aires, as a young working woman in nineteen-fifties Boston, she had been known for dressing well on very little money; and she and her brother had managed to support their widowed mother, too. But Lucienne was well over sixty now, and perhaps this turquoise dress she'd bought for a friend's grandson's bar mitzvah was too bright for the present company. Perhaps it was also too tight for what Lucienne called her few extra pounds and Harry called her blessed corpulence. He was a fatty himself.

In the da Costas' disciplined presence Harry was always a little embarrassed about their appetites, his and Lucienne's. Certainly they had nothing else to be ashamed of: not a thing! They were well-educated, as high-school teachers had had to be in their day (she'd taught French, he chemistry). Lucienne spoke three languages, four if you counted Yiddish. Harry conversed only in Brooklyn English, but he understood Lucienne in all of her tongues. They subscribed to *The New Yorker* and *Science* and *American Heritage*.

These da Costas, though—they were very tall, they were very thin. Judith with her pewter hair and dark clothing could have passed for a British governess. Justin was equally daunting: a high brow, and a lean nose, and thin lips always forming meaningful expressions. But there were moments when Justin glanced at Judith while speaking, and a spasm of anxiety crossed his face, getting entangled with the meaningful expressions. Then Justin and Harry briefly became allies: two younger brothers who'd been caught smoking. One morning at breakfast Harry had described this occasional feeling of kinship to his wife. Lucienne looked at him for a while, then got up and went around the table and kissed him.

Paprika breadsticks! The waiter's young hand shook as he lowered the basket. Judith took none; Justin took one but didn't bite; Lucienne took one and began to munch; Harry took one and then parked another behind his ear.

"Ha," said Judith mirthlessly.

"Ha ha," said Justin.

Lucienne looked at Harry, and sighed, and smiled—her wide motherly smile, reminding him of the purpose of this annual evening out. He removed the breadstick, brushing possible crumbs from his shoulder. "What do you hear from our kids?" he said to Justin.

"Our kids love it out there in Santa Fe. I don't share their taste for the high and dry," Justin said with an elegant shrug.

"You're a Yankee from way back," said Harry.

The da Costas, as Harry well knew, were an old Portuguese-

Dutch family who had begun assimilating the minute they arrived in the New World—in 1800, something like that—and had intermarried whenever an Episcopalian would have them. Fifty years ago Justin studied medicine for the purpose of learning psychiatry. His practice still flourished. He saw patients in a free-standing office, previously a stable, behind their home, previously a farmhouse, the whole compound fifteen miles north of Boston. Judith had designed all the conversions. The windows of Justin's consulting room faced a soothing stand of birches.

The Savitskys had visited the da Costas once, three years ago, the night before Miriam Savitsky's wedding to Jotham da Costa. At that party they discovered that there were back yards in Greater Boston through which rabbits ran, into which deer tripped; that people in the mental health professions did not drink hard liquor (Justin managed to unearth a bottle of Scotch from a recess under the sink); and that the severe Judith was the daughter of a New Jersey pharmacist. The pharmacist was there on the lawn, in a deck chair: aged and garrulous. Harry and his new son-in-law's grandfather talked for a while about synthetic serotonin. The old man had died last winter.

Cocktails! The Hussar did provide Scotch, perhaps knowing no better. The fiddler's repertoire descended into the folk—some Russian melodies. Harry guessed that Lucienne knew their Yiddish lyrics. The da Costas ignored the tunes. They were devotees of Early Music. To give them their due—and Harry always tried to give them their due—they perhaps did not intend to convey the impression that dining out once a year with the Savitskys was bearable, but only marginally. Have pity, he told himself. Their cosseted coexistence with gentle wildlife must make them uncomfortable with extremes of color, noise, and opinions. And for their underweight Jotham, who still suffered from acne at the age of thirty-seven, they'd probably wanted somebody other than a wide-hipped, dense-haired lawyer with a loud laugh.

"The kids' apartment out there ... it's adorable," said Lucienne.

"With all that clutter, how can anybody tell?" said Harry.

"Mostly Jotham's paints and canvases, that clutter," Justin bravely admitted.

"Miriam drops her briefcase in one room, her pocketbook in another, throws her keys on the toilet tank," said Lucienne. "I raised her wrong," in mock repentance.

"They like their jobs. They both seem happy," said Judith, turning large khaki eyes to Harry—a softened gaze. Justin said, "They do," and Lucienne said "Do," and for a moment, the maitre d' if *he* was looking, the fiddler if he was looking, anybody idly looking, might have taken them for two couples happy with their connection-by-marriage. Sometimes what looked so became so. If Jotham was a bit high-strung for the Savitskys, if Miriam was too argumentative for the da Costas, well, you couldn't have everything. Could you? "Many people have nothing," Harry said aloud, startling Judith, alerting Justin's practiced empathy—"Yes?" the doctor encouraged—and not at all troubling Lucienne, who was on her fifth breadstick.

The appetizers came—four different dishes full of things that could kill you. Each person tasted everything, the Savitskys eager, the da Costas restrained. They talked about the Red Sox, at least the Savitskys did. The team had begun the season well, and would break their hearts as always, wait and see. The da Costas murmured something.

The main course arrived, and a bottle of wine. Judith poured: everyone got half a glass. They talked about the gubernatorial race. The da Costas were staunch Democrats, though it sometimes pained them. "No one cares enough about the environment," said Judith. Harry nodded—he didn't care about the environment at all.

The fiddler fiddled. They talked about Stalin—there was a new biography. None of them had read it, and so conversation rested easily on the villainy they already knew.

Harry finished the rest of the wine.

They talked about movies that both couples had seen, though of course not together.

There were some silences.

Lucienne would tell the story tonight, Harry thought.

She would tell the story soon. The da Costas had never heard the story. She had been waiting, as she always did, for the quiet moment, the calm place, the inviting question, and the turning point in a growing intimacy.

Harry had heard the story scores of times. He had heard it in Yiddish and in French and occasionally in Spanish. Mostly, though, she told it in her lightly accented English.

He had heard the story in many places. In the sanctuary of the synagogue her voice fluted from the bima. She was sitting on a Survivor Panel, that time. She wasn't technically a Survivor, had never set foot in a Camp, but still. He'd heard it in living rooms, on narrow back-yard decks, in porches attached to beachfront bungalows, in restaurants like The Hussar. Once—the only instance, to his knowledge, she'd awarded the story to a stranger—he'd heard it in the compartment of an Irish train; their companion was a priest, who listened with deep attention. Once she'd told it at the movies. They and another couple arrived early by mistake and had to occupy half an hour while Trivia questions lingered on the screen. That night she had narrated from his left, leaning toward their friends—a pair of Lesbian teachers—on his right. While she spoke she stared at them with the usual intensity. Harry, kept in place by his wife aslant his lap, stared at *her*: her pretty profile, her apricot hair, the flesh lapping from her chin.

Whatever language she employed, the nouns were unadorned, the syntax plain, the vocabulary undemanding: not a word that couldn't be understood by children, though she never told the story to children, unless you counted Miriam.

He could tell the thing himself, in any of her tongues.

I was four. The Nazis had taken over. We were desperate to escape. My father went out every morning—to stand in line at one place or another, to try to pay the right person.

That morning—he took my brother with him. My brother was twelve. They went to one office and were on their way to a second. Soldiers in helmets grabbed my father. My brother saw the truck then, and the people on it, crying. The soldiers pushed my father toward the truck. "And your son, too." One of them took my brother by the sleeve of his coat.

My father stopped, then. The soldier kept yanking him. "Son?" my father said. "That kid isn't my son. I don't even know him." The German still held on to my brother. My father turned away from them both, and started walking again toward the truck. My brother saw one shoulder lift in a shrug. He heard his voice. "Some Goy," my father said.

So they let my brother go. He came running home, and he showed us the ripped place on his sleeve where they had held him. We managed to get out that night. We went to Holland, and got on a boat for Argentina.

The dessert came. Four different sweets: again they shared.

Lucienne said, "We will go to Santa Fe for the Holidays."

Judith said, "We will go for Thanksgiving."

"And the kids will come East for... in December," said Justin.

The young couple spent half their vacation with one set of parents, half with the other. "More room in their place," Miriam told Harry and Lucienne. "More food here."

The bill came. They paid with credit cards. The nervous waiter hurried to bring their outerwear—two overcoats, and Judith's down jacket, and Lucienne's fur stole inherited from her mother.

"Judith," said Lucienne. "I forgot to mention your father's death."

"You sent a kind note," said Judith in a final manner.

"My own father died when I was a little girl," said Lucienne. "But when my mother died—I was fifty, already—then I felt truly forlorn, an orphan."

"Dad's life satisfied him," said Judith.

The fiddler had paused. A quiet moment. Justin leaned toward Lucienne.

"You were a little girl?" he said softly. "What did your father die of?"

The patrons were devotedly eating. A calm place. A growing intimacy.

"Where?" he asked.

She lifted one shoulder, and lifted her lip too. "Overseas," she said. She stood up and wrapped herself in her ratty stole; and Harry had to run a little, she was so fast getting to the door.

Joshua Dalsimer

THE AUTHOR

Edith Pearlman has published over one hundred stories in national magazines, literary journals, anthologies, and online publications. Her work has appeared in *The Best American Short Stories*, *The O. Henry Prize* collection, *New Stories from the South: The Year's Best*, and *The Pushcart Prize* collection. Her first collection of stories, *Vaquita*, won the Drue Heinz Prize for Literature, and her second, *Love Among The Greats*, won the Spokane Prize for Fiction.

Pearlman's short essays have appeared in the *The Atlantic Monthly*, *The Smithsonian Magazine*, *Preservation Magazine*, and *Yankee*. Her travel writing—about the Cotswolds, Budapest, Jerusalem, Paris, and Tokyo—has been published in *The New York Times* and elsewhere; but she is a New Englander by birth and preference. She grew up in Providence, Rhode Island, and now lives with her husband in Brookline, Massachusetts. She has two grown children.

Edith Pearlman has worked in a computer firm and a soup kitchen; she has served in Brookline's Town Meeting; her hobbies are reading, walking, and matchmaking.